Courage Bay Sentinel

Avenger Linked to Latest Murder

Courage Bay's serial killer appears to have struck again.

Businessman Bernie Brusco, who survived a recent murder attempt at a private fund-raiser for the Courage Bay Hospital, was found dead Sunday night at the base of a cliff backing onto his home in the exclusive neighborhood of Jacaranda Heights. Brusco's death has been labeled a homicide by police, but so far Chief Max Zirinsky will not confirm that this case is being treated as yet another killing by the Avenger.

Brusco, who moved here recently from Los Angeles, collapsed from an apparent heart attack at the society fund-raiser last Friday night. Chief of staff Callie Baker, who was also in attendance, applied CPR on-site until the ambulance arrived. Doctors at Courage Bay Hospital discovered Brusco had been given a drink laced with the drug ephedra. Once Brusco was released from hospital, it appears that his killer came back to finish the job.

Chief Zirinsky keeps assuring the public that there is no need for alarm, but the citizens of Courage Bay can't help asking the question "Who will the Avenger hit next?"

About the Author

code RED

JOANNA WAYNE

is the bestselling, award-winning author of thirty-two novels. Joanna is known for her fast pacing and cutting-edge suspense, as well as her skill at creating believable and passionate relationships between memorable characters. HIDDEN PASSIONS is her latest series from Harlequin Intrigue. These stories are set in towns and cities across the southern part of the United States where suspense awaits around every corner, and passion is as hot and sultry as the settings. Joanna also has written several novellas for anthologies, and books for the TRUEBLOOD TEXAS, FORRESTER SQUARE and CODE RED continuity series. Her first single title, *Alligator Moon,* was released in June of 2004. Joanna loves to hear from readers and encourages them to write to her at Joanna@JoannaWayne.com.

CODE RED

JOANNA WAYNE

JUSTICE FOR ALL

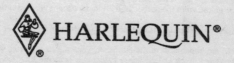

HARLEQUIN®

TORONTO • NEW YORK • LONDON
AMSTERDAM • PARIS • SYDNEY • HAMBURG
STOCKHOLM • ATHENS • TOKYO • MILAN • MADRID
PRAGUE • WARSAW • BUDAPEST • AUCKLAND

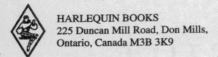

HARLEQUIN BOOKS
225 Duncan Mill Road, Don Mills,
Ontario, Canada M3B 3K9

ISBN 0-373-61295-8

JUSTICE FOR ALL

Copyright © 2004 by Harlequin Books S.A.

Joanna Wayne is acknowledged as the author of this work

www.eHarlequin.com

Printed in U.S.A.

Dear Reader,

The world is always in need of heroes. That's why I was so excited about participating in a series that concentrated on the heroic efforts of firefighters, police officers, medical personnel and other citizens of Courage Bay. Max Zirinsky and Callie Baker are the epitome of true heroes to me, in that they risked extreme danger to themselves to do what had to be done to stop the Avenger.

And I especially liked that the series was set in California. As a Southerner, I don't get to the West Coast nearly often enough, but I was fortunate enough to spend several summers there a few years back. Many moments stand out in my mind from those visits, but some of my favorites involve sunsets and moonlit walks on the beach—as romantic a spot as I could ever wish for. I could almost feel the sand between my toes and hear the roar of the surf when Max and Callie took their first walk along the beach. I hope you do as well.

I love to hear from readers. Please visit my Web site at www.joannawayne.com. And let me know if you'd like to be added to my newsletter list.

Happy reading,

Joanna

In memory of my good friend Linda West,
aka Linda Lewis and Dixie Kane,
who warmed many a heart
with her tales of love and laughter.

CHAPTER ONE

THE GALA WAS IN FULL SWING, as glitzy an affair as socialite and heiress Mary McGuire Hancock, III, was known for. White canvas canopied the spacious grounds, strands of miniature lights twinkled like stars in every tree and music from a jazz combo played backup to conversations and laughter.

And like all gatherings of the Courage Bay elite, fashion was on parade. Sequined gowns clung to gorgeously slinky bodies and stretched across paunchier ones. Men in tuxedos lined up at the open bars, while waiters in stiff white shirts and creased black pants wandered the crowd with trays of recherche hors d'oeuvres.

It was a night for visiting old friends and making new ones, a night for schmoozing and soliciting checks for impressive sums of money.

A night for murder.

His pulse quickened at the thought, but he was careful not to show any sign of his excitement. This had to be just another charitable function until the perfect moment presented itself. The night had just started. He had plenty of time.

But once he struck, justice would be swift and merciless. Most importantly, justice would be served.

CALLIE BAKER FINISHED a conversation with one of the councilmen and turned to find District Attorney Henry Lalane at her elbow.

"You look lovely tonight, Callie."

"Thank you, Henry."

"This must be a big event for the hospital's chief of staff."

"Bigger for the children who'll benefit from the donations we raise," she said. "The money's earmarked to purchase new equipment for the pediatric wing."

"It's a great turnout."

"You have to love that about Courage Bay. Rich or poor, the residents are always ready to support a worthy cause."

"There's not a lot of poor people here tonight."

"No, but there have been so many other fund-raisers across the city. The latest was sponsored by the students at Jacaranda High. They raised over a thousand dollars for the hospital at their spring carnival."

"So I heard. My niece goes to school there."

And his daughter probably would have been a student there, too, if she hadn't been killed a few years before in a random drive-by shooting. No one was ever apprehended for the crime. Callie was sorry she'd mentioned the school now, though Henry didn't seem upset by the comment. Still, she knew how devastated he and his wife had been at the loss of their daughter.

Henry sipped his drink. "Bernie Brusco seems to be enjoying himself," he said, letting his gaze settle on the man who was laughing and tangoing across the portable dance floor with their hostess.

"Not the best of dancers," Callie observed, "but he's generous. I hadn't met him before tonight, but he wrote out a very substantial check for the hospital."

"He should. He's probably one of the richest men here."

"Really. I wouldn't have guessed that. What does he do?"

"Owns a string of convenience stores in L.A. Yet here he is crashing our little social scene."

"Mary said he bought a house in Courage Bay."

"Lucky us."

"And that must be another new face in town," Callie said, nodding toward a very handsome man standing beneath a palm tree a few yards away, looking exceedingly bored. "I've never seen him before."

"Looks like an aging surfer to me. I hate those new T-shirt looking things that pass for dress shirts."

"It's the style." Callie had no idea if the stranger surfed, but she thought he was aging quite nicely. Probably near forty, he was still lean and sun-bronzed, with short sandy hair and a great body. The kind of guy Callie's best friend Mikki would classify as a hunk.

Too bad Mikki hadn't been available to attend the party. She'd have made certain the guy wasn't bored, unless he happened to have a ring on his finger. Mikki's claim was that every good-looking guy in southern California was gay, married or divorced and carried more baggage than a 747. Callie wasn't totally convinced she was wrong.

"Think I'll go introduce myself," Henry said. "Then I'll have to search for my social butterfly wife. It's getting late, and I've got a full day tomorrow."

"Are you working on Saturdays now?"

"Too many of them, but not by choice. The workload seems to have doubled over the last year. Unfortunately our staff hasn't."

Callie nodded and finished her second glass of champagne as Henry walked away. She spent the next few minutes chatting with various guests, then decided she was too tired to make small talk. It was nearing midnight, and like Henry, she was feeling the strain of a long, busy week. Most of the doctors on staff at Courage Bay Hospital who'd attended the event had already called it an evening.

Callie headed toward the area where she'd seen Mary and Bernie a few minutes earlier, wanting to thank her hostess one last time before cutting out. She stopped short when she heard a ruckus break out beneath the canopy to her left. She spun around just in time to see Bernie Brusco fall against one of the small tables. Another guest tried to break his fall, but the table collapsed, and both men fell on top of it.

"We need a doctor," someone yelled.

Callie rushed over, along with everyone else in hearing distance. She ordered the anxious crowd back and knelt in the grass beside Bernie.

"Can't...breathe. Chest...hurts."

"Call 911 for an ambulance," Callie ordered, directing her comment to Mary. She reached for Bernie's wrist to check his pulse. It was dangerously accelerated.

"Do something." Bernie's voice was a hoarse whisper.

Callie put the flat of her hand on the man's chest and felt the rapid, irregular beating of his heart. "Has this happened before?"

"No."

His shallow gasps weren't getting much oxygen to his lungs, so she slipped her arm beneath him and placed his head at an angle that should have made breathing easier. He clutched her arm and held on tight.

"Don't let...me die."

"I won't." Not if she could help it. "Try to take a deep breath."

"I'm...trying."

He gasped then went limp.

"Is he dead?" an onlooker asked.

Callie didn't bother to answer, just leaned over and gave a sharp whack to Bernie's chest with the side of her hand, then pressed his heart between the sternum and the spine with rhythmic motions. Thankfully the heart responded and started beating again on its own. The pulse remained high, inconsistent with a typical heart attack.

The ambulance arrived in short order. "His pulse is near 180," Callie told the paramedics as they loaded him onto the stretcher. "Squirt some procardra under his tongue when you get him in the ambulance. I'll call the E.R. and alert them you're on the way and to have an IV setup for a nipride drip."

Bernie managed to murmur his thanks to Callie as the medics hurried him to the ambulance.

Mary was waiting at Callie's side when she finished the phone call to the E.R. "Will he be all right?" she asked, her voice shaky.

"The hospital E.R. is one of the finest in the state. He'll get excellent care." It was the best she could promise.

Mary blinked and flicked the back of her hand across her eyes. "Poor Bernie. One minute he was really enjoying himself, wolfing down hors d'oeuvres as if he hadn't eaten for days and drinking some kind of specialty cocktail the bartender had mixed for him. The next he was gasping for breath."

"Which bartender mixed his drink?"

"One of those young men," Mary answered, motioning to the portable serving area set up at the back of the tent.

"What was he eating?"

"The seafood canapés—you know, the ones served on the shrimp-shaped crackers. He'd piled a dozen or so on his plate. Couldn't stop raving about how good they were." Mary slapped her hand against her cheek.

"Oh, dear. You don't suppose they made him sick, do you? My caterer insists on the freshest ingredients. I'm certain the seafood wasn't tainted."

"If it was tainted, we'd have a lot more people than Bernie affected. But it's possible he had an allergic reaction to one of the ingredients."

"It looked like a heart attack to me," Mary said, "but then he's only forty-five, and he seemed perfectly healthy before he collapsed."

Callie scanned the immediate area for his glass or perhaps a half eaten seafood canapé but found neither. No doubt both had been removed by one of the attentive waiters.

"I guess I'd better get back to the guests and try to salvage what's left of the party spirit," Mary said, clasping and unclasping her hands. "I don't feel much like it, though. I thought Bernie was going to die right here in the grass. I don't know what I would have done if you hadn't been here."

"But I was here, and he didn't die," Callie said, taking one of Mary's hand in hers and giving it a comforting squeeze. "The party was lovely, and what happened to Bernie wasn't your fault."

"Will you call me as soon as you know something? I can come and stay with Bernie if you think he needs me."

"I'll call, but he's probably better off without company tonight."

Callie waited until Mary walked away, then went to the large serving table, took a couple of the seafood ca-

napés and wrapped them in a paper napkin. She stopped
and had the young bartender write out the ingredients
he'd used in Bernie's special drink, as well.

Avoiding as many of the guests as she could, Callie
walked to the front lawn of the sprawling estate and
waited for one of the attendants to get her car. The bored
stranger was waiting for his as well.

"You were impressive," he said, stepping closer. "I
noticed you earlier but would never have taken the beautiful woman in red for a doctor."

"Difficult to recognize us when we're not wearing
our white coats," Callie said. "I don't think we've met."
She extended her hand. "I'm Callie Baker, chief of staff
at Courage Bay Hospital."

"Jerry Hawkins."

"Are you new to the area?"

"Visiting my mother, Abby Hawkins."

"I didn't know Abby had a son."

"I'm the black sheep of the family. Mother usually
keeps me hidden away when I come to visit, lest I embarrass her in front of her friends."

"Then she should be proud of you. You behaved quite
appropriately tonight."

"I have my moments."

The attendant drove up with his car. Jerry started to
walk away, then turned back to Callie. "The world
would have been a better place if you'd let him die."

"Excuse me?"

"You do know how Bernie Brusco makes his money,

don't you?"

"I heard he owns a chain of convenience stores."

"To launder the cash he makes supplying drugs to half of southern California."

"What makes you think that?"

"Not a matter of thinking it. It's fact."

"Even if what you say is true, it wouldn't have mattered. I took an oath to save lives. All lives, not just the ones I deem worthy."

"Too bad. You probably sentenced a few hundred adolescents to death by keeping Brusco alive." He turned and walked to his car, leaving the sting of his accusation hanging in the still night air.

MAX ZIRINSKY BIT the end off a cold French fry and stared at the names he'd scribbled on the napkin. Dylan Deeb, Bruce Nepom, Lorna Sinke and Carlos Esposito. Four unsolved murders in one year. Different MO in every case but with one common factor. They were all suspected of having committed a criminal act.

Max reviewed the evidence in his mind, the way he did dozens of times a day. Deeb had made one hit movie, which was preceded and then followed by a string of marginal successes and a few bombs. He'd bought a home in Courage Bay after the box office hit, claiming he'd wanted a place where he could flee the Hollywood publicity circus.

More often than not, he'd brought the circus with him, to the disdain of his privacy-loving neighbors.

Deeb was known for his wild parties and a parade of very young, big breasted babes who came and went, frequently in groups.

He'd been brought up on charges of soliciting sexual favors from underage female actresses in exchange for parts in his movies. But all Deeb had to do was give his unhappy starlets the promise of a role in one of his movies, and they merely smiled and refused to testify. Deeb was scum, but he'd walked away from the charges a free man.

Someone had changed that by paying a visit to Deeb's Courage Bay house in the midst of one of the worst series of rains to hit the area in years. Warnings had gone out for everyone in the area to evacuate.

Deeb's house had been swept away in a mud slide with Deeb still inside it. Severe bruising on his neck indicated foul play, and an autopsy revealed that he'd been strangled before his house had taken the plunge.

Then there was Bruce Nepom. An unlicensed contractor, Nepom was taken to the E.R. at Courage Bay Hospital after his roof collapsed on him during the storm of the century back in January. Nepom died while in hospital, and an autopsy showed his injuries stemmed from trauma to the base of his skull with a blunt instrument. He'd been facing possible charges in the death of an elderly couple after the roof he'd built for them collapsed, but the case was dropped due to lack of evidence.

The third case involved an aide to city council named Lorna Sinke. The woman had escaped prosecution in the death of her elderly parents when evidence was ruled inadmissible after an improperly executed search warrant. Sinke had been shot in a hostage situation at city hall and died later in the hospital.

And finally there was Esposito, a scumbag who abducted Mexican children from their families and put them to work as migrant workers. Esposito had died instantly when his small plane had crashed into the ballroom of the Grand Hotel. An investigation had found evidence that someone had deliberately tampered with the plane's engine.

Bottom line was that some damned avenger was creating a crime wave of his own and he was doing it right under Max's nose. That would have been tough if he was still just a detective on the homicide squad. But now that he was chief of police, it was driving him over the edge.

"Want another beer?" Jake asked, wiping a wet spot off the bar just left of Max's elbow.

"Nah. I've had enough."

"You've only had two. It's Friday night. Live a little."

"I'm living, hip hoppin' big time. Just keeping a low profile so it doesn't make everyone else jealous."

Jake leaned over the bar and stared at the names Max had printed on the napkin. "If you were living, those would be foxes' names and phone numbers on that wrinkled old napkin, not victims."

"Victims are easier to deal with. They don't expect flowers."

"But women have curves and don't smell like those sweaty cops you were talking to earlier tonight."

"Could be, but the cops will still respect me in the morning."

"That's not funny, Max."

And not true, either. If the department didn't solve these murder cases, no one was going to respect him in the morning, least of all himself.

He glanced at his watch. Nearly 1:00 a.m., and he was still wide-awake. Not much point going back to his empty apartment and tossing around in that king-size bed all by himself. "Okay, Jake, one more beer."

"You got it, Max. The night is young. And you see that table of hotties sitting over there sipping margaritas..."

Max swivelled around on the bar stool and stared at the three young women flirting with a couple of the department's newer and fortunately unmarried recruits sitting at the table next to them.

"I see them. Now what?"

"Hell, Max. Do I have to tell you everything? Send them a drink. Go over and talk to them. You might just get lucky tonight."

"I'm old enough to be their father."

"But you aren't their father."

"If I was, I'd tell them to stay the hell away from those cops they're working so hard to pick up. Cops make lousy husbands."

Jake shook his head and walked away. By the time he returned with the beer, Max was deep in thought about getting lucky. Luck for him would be arresting the Avenger—before he struck again.

CALLIE FINISHED WRITING out the orders for a thorough toxicology check on Bernie, handed it to the nurse on duty and walked back to the small cubicle where the patient was stretched out on the examining table. Ordinarily the E.R. doctor who had taken charge of Bernie when he arrived at the hospital would take over at this point, but Callie had decided to be Bernie's doctor of record since she'd treated him at Mary's.

"So how much longer do I have to stay here?" Bernie asked, shifting his weight to his right side and sticking one bare foot from beneath the bleached white sheet.

"Only about ten more minutes in here, but I'm admitting you to the hospital."

"Don't even think about it." He waved his hand as if dismissing her last statement. "I can't stay in the hospital. My business doesn't run itself."

"Which makes it all the more important that you stay here long enough for us to find out what caused your problems tonight."

"I know what caused it. Stress. And if I don't get out of here, the stress will double."

"Stress could have brought on tonight's episode," she admitted, "but it's not likely."

"It doesn't matter what caused it. I'm fine now," he

insisted. "I saw my blood pressure reading. It's 140 over 100. That's practically normal."

"Much closer to normal than it was, but I'd still like to run a few tests, and you need to see a cardiologist."

"So, what are we looking at? One day?"

"Possibly. Maybe more depending on when a cardiologist can see you and what kind of results we get from the tests."

He rolled his eyes. "I have to be out of here by Monday morning at the latest."

"I say we discuss that after we know more. I'm going to limit the number of visitors you can have to two at a time, fifteen minutes a visit, four times a day. You need to get some rest."

"Fine by me. I don't want people hanging around gawking at me hanging out of this thing." He pulled on the loose fabric of the hospital gown to make his point.

She made a few notations on his chart, told him she'd see him in the morning and stepped out the door, shedding her white lab coat as she did.

"Hey, no one told me they were filming E.R. here tonight. If they had, I would have dressed for the occasion, too."

Callie turned to see Mikki McCallister striding toward her. "What are you doing here at this time of night?"

"One of my darlings started running a high fever and his parents were nervous wrecks. I told them I'd meet them here and check him out."

"Have you seen the patient yet?"

"Just left them. He's got one of those stubborn viruses that don't realize they're supposed to check out after twenty-four hours. He'll be fine, just needed the special touch of Dr. Mikki—and some glucose. What about you? Did you miss us so much you had to leave the soiree and pay a visit to the emergency room?"

"You got it. I think it's the ambiance around here I can't stay away from. Impatient patients. Harried doctors. And that woman yelling in Room 4 because we won't keep supplying her with pain pills for her imaginary ailments."

"So why *are* you here?" Mikki asked.

"One of the guests at the party collapsed and his heart stopped beating. I had to manually pump the chest to get it going again, so I stopped by to check on him."

"Heart attack?"

"Atypical symptoms. It's possible it was an allergic reaction, maybe to something he ate or drank at the party."

"Speaking of food, I'm famished. How about stopping off at the Bar and Grill with me for a burger? You can wow the night crew with your cleavage."

"Wowing Jake the bartender. Now why didn't I think of that?"

Mikki was talking nonstop, but Callie's mind stayed on Bernie as they walked to their cars.

The world would have been a better place if you'd let him die.

If Jerry Hawkins thought that, then others probably

did, too—like the man that both the press and the police dubbed the Avenger. But would a serial killer be
crazy enough to attempt murder at a house with nearly
a hundred people milling around?

"Meet you in the bar," Mikki said, unlocking her car
door. "And don't look so glum. I'm getting strange vibes
about the rest of the night. Must have something to do
with that knockout dress of yours."

"Your vibes should go on Prozac."

Callie slid behind the wheel, mindful of the red cocktail dress that slid up to mid thigh when she sat. The
dress was a bit more revealing than she usually wore, a
splurge purchase on one of her rare trips to Rodeo Drive.
She'd loved it on the mannequin and liked it even better on her.

But hot dress or not, Mikki's vibes or not, she didn't
expect or want any male attention tonight. Not that she
was opposed to dating, but her recent attempts at relationships had been more trouble than they were worth.
Her last steady had said she was too intimidating. When
she asked what he meant by that, he couldn't—or
wouldn't—explain.

Oh, well. She could live without a man in her life if
she had to. She'd done it for the last eight years. Besides,
she had Pickering to keep her company. He was always
glad to see her and never complained of her long hours
or accused her of being intimidating.

Retrievers were great that way.

Her cell phone rang before she reached the restaurant. It was Mary, anxious for news of her ill guest.

MAX FINISHED THE THIRD beer and pulled his wallet from his pocket. "What do I owe you, Jake?"

"I got your ticket here somewhere." He turned and searched through the collection behind the bar until he found Max's bill. "That will be $14.20… Well, well, well, look what just walked in."

Max pulled out a twenty-dollar bill and slid it across the bar to Jake before turning to see what new babe had caught the roaming eye of the bartender.

It was Callie Baker in red—her cinnamon hair framing her youthful face, her long shapely legs set off by the high-heeled sandals. He swallowed hard as a memory of Callie flashed in his mind. A brief encounter that should never have happened.

But the old memory showed no sign of retreating as Callie waved and started walking in his direction. He should have left a beer ago.

CHAPTER TWO

"IS SITTING AT THE BAR OKAY?" Callie asked, once she'd spotted Max. She hadn't planned to go to him just yet with her suspicions, but since he was here, she'd like to hear his opinions on Bernie Brusco.

"That's not a bar stool kind of dress you're wearing, but it works for me," Mikki said. "Grab us a seat. I see my one of my firemen buddies standing by the pool table. I want to go over and say hi."

"I thought you were famished."

"I am. Order me a cheeseburger, loaded, including jalapeños, and add a side of chili fries."

"You're eating hot peppers and chili fries in the middle of the night?"

"Sure. I'm from Texas. We like it spicy—the hotter the better."

"Guess that explains your fondness for firemen."

Mikki smiled as she strode off, her long blond hair bouncing about her shoulders. Now that she'd shed her lab coat, she looked more like a teenager than a doctor.

Callie walked over and stopped at Max's elbow. "Mind if I join you?"

"I don't know." He gave her outfit an approving once-over. "Is Prince Charming going to show up and demand a duel?"

"No Prince Charming. I was at a fund-raiser earlier and had to stop back by the hospital. I didn't bother to change." She sidled onto the stool next to him.

"Can't get away from work even on a Friday night. You're getting as bad as me."

"I tried. Bernie Brusco collapsed at the party. I stopped by the E.R. to check on him."

"Is he all right?" Max asked.

"I think so. Actually it was more serious than a collapse. His heart stopped beating." She hooked the back of her heels on the rung of the bar stool. "Do you know Bernie?"

"We haven't met, but I know who he is and that he bought a house in Jacaranda Heights."

"What else do you know about him?"

"Nothing officially."

"How about unofficially?" Callie asked.

"Like what?"

"Is he into drug trafficking?"

"I'm guessing that's not the occupation he put on his hospital admittance form."

"No, but someone at the party seemed convinced it was true."

"He's the kingpin," Max admitted. "Runs his own little cocaine and crack empire. L.A. police have arrested him several times, but the charges never stick. There's no sign he's involved in distribution in Courage Bay, though. Guess he doesn't want to dirty up his own back-yard." Max rested his elbows on the bar. "Was his collapse drug related?"

"It's possible. I ordered a toxicology report."

Jake took the order for Callie's glass of wine and Mikki's feast.

"How about you, Chief Zirinsky?" he asked. "Can I get you another beer?"

Max waved him off. "I've had my limit." He waited until Jake walked away before continuing the discussion. "Any chance he was poisoned?"

"A chance, but no real reason to suspect it at this point."

Max nodded, but she could tell by his expression that the wheels in his mind were still rolling. He thought this might be the work of the Avenger. Not that she hadn't considered it. In fact, she'd found herself leery of every death or unexplained accident since she'd alerted Max of the suspicious nature of Bruce Nepom's injuries. Still, she didn't have any medical information yet to indicate intentional poisoning.

"There's a lot of things that could have caused the symptoms, Max. Don't read too much into this yet."

"It's a waste of time to tell that to a cop on a murder case, Callie. We read too much into everything."

"Sounds as if you don't have any real leads yet on the Avenger."

"Try *no* leads. When will you have the results back on the blood test?"

"Tomorrow morning. I can call you if you like."

"Please do."

"The party was at Mary Hancock's, a very top-drawer affair. I can't imagine any of the guests capable of serial murder, even in the name of justice."

"Wouldn't have to be a guest who poisoned him," Max said. "There had to be lots of other people around as well. Caterers, bartenders, food servers, parking attendants, cleanup crew."

Jake set Callie's glass of wine in front of her, and she picked it up and took a long, cooling sip. The talk of murder was getting to her.

"So what else is going on in your life these days, Dr. Callie Baker?" Max asked, obviously sensing her increasing uneasiness.

"Mostly work—and taking Pickering for his beach walks."

"I guess being chief of staff adds more to your plate."

"Some. I've stopped taking on new patients for now, but I'm still seeing all my established ones. What about you?"

"Work, work and more work."

"Guess we're a couple of duds," Callie said.

"A dud? Not you, Callie. You make the society section of the local paper at least once a month."

"What are you doing reading the society section, Max? You were never interested in the social whirl."

"I check out the hot women."

"You could have your pick of women in this town, hot or not. You always could."

"You think so?"

"I'm sure of it." The answer took zero thought. Max was not only good-looking in a rugged sort of way, but smart and honest and—and incredibly tender, though most women probably didn't know that.

She hadn't until the night when… Callie's thoughts were thankfully interrupted by Mikki's boisterous arrival.

"Hey, no food yet? What's the holdup, Jake?" Mikki took the stool next to Callie's. "A woman could starve in this place."

"Keeping it hot for you," Jake answered.

"Max Zirinsky, meet Dr. Mikki McCallister," Callie said, making the introductions. "Mikki is a pediatrician on staff at the hospital. Max is Courage Bay's chief of police."

The two of them reached across Callie and shook hands just as Jake arrived with the food.

"I'll get out of here and let you two party on," Max said.

"There's always room for one more at a party," Mikki offered.

"No, we've already established I'm a dud."

"We did no such thing," Callie chided. "We only established the fact that you work too much."

Max stood and placed a hand on Callie's shoulder. The touch sent a shiver of awareness shimmying through her system. That's what she got for letting those old memories creep back into her mind.

"I'll call you in the morning," she said. "Will you be home?"

"Call my cell." He picked up a napkin and scribbled the number on it. "It was good seeing you. You look great."

"Thanks. You, too."

He said a quick goodbye to Mikki, then headed for the door, his cop swagger as pronounced as ever.

"Did I just break up a magical moment?" Mikki asked.

"Whatever gave you that idea?"

"I sensed a sizzle."

"No way. Max is an old friend."

"Doesn't look that old to me, and he does great things for a pair of jeans. Terrific butt."

"Do you check out every guy that way?"

"Like you didn't. I saw you watching him walk off. But I'm more interested in that phone number he scribbled down for you, and the way he was eyeing you when he told you how good you looked. I could feel the heat over here."

"That was fumes from the chili."

"So, what's the story on him?"

"Max is an old friend, just like I said. And my ex's cousin."

"Tell me more."

"That's it. Max and Tony are probably as opposite as two people can be, but they're kin. And the phone number is so I can let him know about a patient whose symptoms seem a little suspicious."

"Playing detective again?"

"Just being cautious."

Mikki picked up her overstuffed burger and some-how got her small mouth opened wide enough to take a chunk out of it. Watching her eat never failed to amaze Callie. Mikki was five-two and couldn't possibly weigh much over a hundred pounds, but she had the appetite of a teenage boy. And the energy of one as well.

She was also an excellent pediatrician and very insightful. But this time she'd definitely misread the signs. Max had come to Callie's rescue once, but he'd backed miles away after that and let her know in silent but certain terms that he had no interest in her as a woman.

Callie let the memory of being in his arms slip into her mind for one heated second, then pushed it back to the hidden crevice where she planned to leave it.

CALLIE LOOKED UP when Dr. Alec Giroux tapped on her open office door. "Mind if I come in? I'm bearing gifts, that is, if you can call a toxicology report a gift."

"Then by all means come in. It's not often I have an E.R. doctor stop in to deliver lab reports."

"Just brown nosing the chief of staff," Alec said.

"Nice try, but you buck me on too many issues for me to buy that. So what's up?"

Alec handed her the lab printout. "I'd walked over to the lab to pick up a report on one of my patients, and the technician brought Bernie Brusco's results to my attention."

"Why is that?"

"His results look a lot like those of the teenager we lost in E.R. last week."

"The ephedra overdose?"

He nodded. "There was a notable amount of ephedra in Bernie's bloodstream as well, along with a trace of cocaine and considerably more than a trace of alcohol."

She scanned the report. "That would explain his symptoms."

"You don't look or sound surprised."

"I've heard that Bernie runs his own drug empire in Los Angeles, so I'm not too shocked that he had the cocaine in his system. He could be selling ephedra, too, since the FDA pulled products containing it from the shelves."

"If he's in the biz, he should have known better than to mix and match volatile drugs."

"You'd think. I'll talk to Max Zirinsky and make him aware of the similarity in the two cases."

"Good idea. And I'll get back to the E.R. Never know what a Saturday morning might bring."

"Just be thankful we're not dealing with a heat wave like the one we had last summer."

"Amen. Never want a summer like that again. A heat wave and a deadly viral epidemic."

An epidemic that had hit Alec particularly hard, since his daughter had almost died from the virus. "How are Cameron and Stacy?" she asked.

"They're great. And Janice has become quite the mother. She's an amazing woman."

He smiled broadly and Callie felt just the tiniest

twinge of envy. Alec's first marriage had been just as big a mistake as hers, but he'd found love again and seemed incredibly happy. Not that Callie wasn't happy. Nor did she have time for a family and children—even if she had been able to have them. A fast growing tumor three years ago had resulted in a hysterectomy.

"Tell Janice hello for me," she said, pushing the unexpected thoughts of family and kids aside.

"Will do."

Callie scanned the lab report again when Alec left, then slipped into her doctor's coat for a personal visit with her patient. Bernie was lucky to be alive, but there was no indication the Avenger had tried to kill him. Looked more like Bernie was trying to save the killer the trouble and do the job himself.

Callie took the elevator up to Bernie's room. The door was open a crack and she heard his boisterous voice and a woman's laughter echoing down the hallway. She tapped lightly on the door before stepping inside.

Mary Hancock stopped laughing and backed away from the bed. "Good morning, Callie. I promise I'm not tiring out the patient. I just came by to check on him and bring him a fruit basket."

"A bit of cheery company won't hurt him, as long as he doesn't overdo it."

Callie spied the fruit basket on the table in the corner of the room. It was covered in cellophane, tied with a gold bow and filled with mangos, avocados, peaches, kiwi and pomegranates, with an impressive pineapple in the middle. The basket was almost as colorful and flamboyant as the bearer.

Mary was one of Callie's patients. At sixty-one, Mary could have easily passed for fifteen years younger. Money for surgery and the right clothes to flatter her petite figure probably took a lot of credit for that, but it was Mary's vivacious personality that added the youthful pizzazz.

Callie pulled the chart at the foot of Bernie's bed. His vitals were back to normal except for a slightly elevated systolic reading. "How are you feeling this morning, Mr. Brusco?"

"Terrific and ready to get out of the hospital. Like I told you, it was just stress. A good night's rest did the trick."

Bernie scooted up higher on his pillow, tugging on the hospital gown so that it didn't pull around the neck. "Thanks for coming by, Mary. And don't worry about me, I'll be fine," he said, dismissing his visitor.

"Good. When you're feeling better, I'll teach you to do the tango correctly."

"With these two left feet?"

They both laughed and Mary said a quick goodbye to Callie before exiting. Mary was obviously fond of Bernie. Callie seriously doubted she knew how the man made his living or that he did drugs himself.

Courage Bay was a few miles and a world away from Los Angeles. In spite of a growing population, the city had a small-town attitude, and people tended to trust one another to be who and what they purported to be. She'd hate to see Mary hurt by a man like Bernie.

"Guess you have the results of the blood work," Bernie said, once Mary was out of the r█

"Just got it back from the lab a fe█ █nutes ago."

"Then you know I had a little cocaine in my system." She nodded.

"I hope you won't get the wrong idea. It's not like I'm an addict or anything. You know how it is up in Los Angeles. You go with the boys, you sniff a little to be sociable. I won't even do that again after what happened last night."

"You had cocaine, alcohol and dangerous levels of an illegal stimulant in your system. That's a pretty lethal mix. You're lucky to be alive this morning."

Bernie narrowed his eyes. "What stimulant?"

A strange question, Callie thought. He'd readily admitted the cocaine, so why not the stimulant? "Ephedra," she said. "A much larger dose than if you'd taken it as a dietary supplement."

"Ephedra." He repeated the word, then drew his lips together and nodded as if he were figuring out a mystery. "You're sure about that?"

"Very sure. Don't you remember taking it?"

"My recollection of last night's activities are not too keen."

That was believable, yet he remembered the party and the cocaine.

He sat up straighter. "You know, Doc, pretty as you are and as nice as the nurses are treating me, I need to get out of here today."

"I recommend you stay until Monday."

"Nothing personal, Doc, but I've got urgent business to take care of. I have to be back in Los Angeles by Monday morning."

"Then at least stay one more night."

He drew his lips into a slight scowl. "One more night, but that's it, no matter what any new tests show."

"It's your choice."

"Thanks, Doc. For last night and for looking in on me today."

"You're welcome, but I can only do so much. The real responsibility for taking care of yourself rests with you."

"Don't I know it."

She made a couple of notations on his chart, slipped it back in place, then told him she'd see him later.

"You're sure about the ephedra?" he asked as she headed for the door.

"I'm sure."

She hurried to the elevator, eager to go back to her office and call Max with the findings. She had no proof at all, but she had a strong hunch that Bernie didn't knowingly take the ephedra. Which meant the Avenger may well have been at Mary's party, armed with the stimulant that had almost killed Bernie Brusco.

MAX PICKED CALLIE UP in front of the hospital at ten after twelve, determined to have no recurrence of the lust that had blindsided him last night, lingering long after he'd crawled into his bed. No way could he play in Callie's league. He probably couldn't even get a job as bat boy.

"Have you had lunch?" Max asked, trying not to notice that she looked as ravishing in the pale gray slacks and the yellow cotton blouse as she had in the dynamite dress last night.

"I haven't even had breakfast," she said.

"Then we might as well eat while we talk, unless you'd rather not."

"Lunch sounds good."

"So where's your preference?" Max asked.

"Somewhere outside. It's much too gorgeous to be stuck indoors."

"How about Grady's?"

"Perfect."

It would be if they were only going there to eat instead of to discuss a possible link to a vengeful killer who'd outsmarted Max at every turn. Grady's was on the beach and had a large covered deck where patrons had a great view of the bay and could listen to the sounds of the surf. On most days there were enough surfers in the area to provide a side show as well.

Callie gave him the results of the lab report and Bernie's reaction on the drive over. By the time the waitress showed them to a table in the back corner of the deck, possibilities were already streaming though his mind.

"So what's your take on this?" Callie asked, once they'd put in their drink order and had been given a menu.

"I think your hunch could be right. Ephedra doesn't

seem the kind of drug a man like Bernie would mess around with, not with all the serious drugs he has at his disposal. Besides, kingpins like Bernie are rarely big-time users. They need to keep their minds clear to run the business."

Which meant it was very possible someone at Mary Hancock's party slipped the stimulant into his food or drink. If it was the Avenger, and if he was in fact at the party last night, this might be the best lead Max had had since the killing spree started.

"There are a lot more common and probably more effective substances a killer could have used," Callie said. "What would make him choose something like ephedra?"

"Any number of reasons. Availability, personal experience, or he may have gotten the idea from the media attention surrounding the death of the high school student."

"That makes sense," Callie admitted.

"If you hadn't been there and Bernie had died of the presenting symptoms, would his death have been classified a heart attack?"

"Quite possibly."

The waitress returned with Max's coffee and Callie's raspberry iced tea. Max ordered a cheeseburger without even glancing at the menu. Callie decided on the fresh green salad topped with lump crab meat and avocado, dressing on the side.

Another glaring difference between them, Max noted. His taste buds were partial to the routine. Callie's went for more sophisticated fare.

Callie rolled a finger over the condensation on her glass. "If Bernie thinks someone tried to kill him, surely he'll go to the police."

"I wouldn't count on that. A guy like Bernie's more likely to seek out his own revenge." Just what Courage Bay and Max needed. An avenger out to get the Avenger. Sounded like a bad Hollywood script, and even thinking about it gave Max a headache.

They fell silent when the waitress brought the food. But not talking was not necessarily a good thing when he was sitting across a small table from Callie, Max acknowledged. It left him too much time to notice the delicate softness of her hands as she forked bites of salad to her full, pink lips. Too much time to admire the way her breasts pushed against the fabric of her blouse. Too much time to remember the way her body had felt pressed against his.

"What do we do, Max?"

The question flustered him for a second before he realized she wasn't reading his mind and referring to the incriminating thoughts he was entertaining. "You've done your part. It's up to me to try to make sense of it all."

"I don't think I have done my part."

He didn't like the sound of that or the look in her eyes right now. "I appreciate the heads-up on this, Callie, but don't even think about getting involved in the investigation."

"Why not? I was standing a few feet away from Bernie when he collapsed. And the hostess is a friend of mine."

"If the Avenger is involved in this, and I'm not even suggesting that he is, we're talking about a man who's killed at least four people and tried to kill Bernie. He's smart and he's dangerous."

"And needs to be stopped."

"Right. By the cops. Not by beautiful doctors with no experience in law enforcement."

"I wasn't planning to start carrying a gun and beating the bushes for the killer."

"Good. Don't talk to Mary about this, either, or anyone else who was at the party."

As he dipped a French fry into a pool of ketchup, it struck Max that this was the first time he'd had lunch with a woman other than the cops on his force in longer than he cared to remember. And he was sitting here giving orders and talking about murder. "I say we drop the subject," he suggested. "It's bad for the digestive system."

"Okay, but I still think I could help with the investigation."

They stopped talking until they finished eating. "So," Callie said, dabbing the napkin to the corner of her lips, "what does the chief of police do for fun on gorgeous Saturday afternoons?"

"Does doing the laundry count as fun?"

She groaned. "Tell me you're joking."

"Of course. That's just the warm-up. It's stopping at the market for TV dinners that really gets my juices pumping. And let me guess. What does the chief of staff at Courage Bay Hospital do? Loll away her hours at the yacht club? Go sailing? Shop for dresses like that sexy little number you had on last night?"

"I'm sailing with friends this afternoon, but every other Saturday I volunteer at the Keller Center. It's a facility that provides housing and medical care for indigent women in their last trimester of pregnancy. Not really what I'd classify as fun, but extremely satisfying."

Her involvement in the center surprised him, though he didn't know why it should. One of the things that had driven her and his cousin apart had been the fact that she chose to work at a clinic in a low income area after completing her residency instead of accepting a very lucrative and prestigious position with a doctor in private practice in Beverly Hills.

The silence grew awkward. It was one of the few times Max envied guys who could make meaningless small talk. Start him on any murder he'd ever investigated and he could talk your ear off. Football, basketball, baseball. Hit him with any of those and he could jump right in. But ask for small talk with a woman and he'd trip right over his tongue.

The waitress stopped by and offered coffee or dessert, but Callie refused both. She was ready to go. Who could blame her? Max pulled a few bills from his money clip and slipped them under the ticket, then stood up to leave.

Callie took a phone call on the drive back and spent the entire trip discussing a cancer patient whose insurance company didn't want to pay for an experimental drug the physician in charge wanted to use. She broke the connection as he pulled into the circular driveway in front of the hospital.

"I enjoyed lunch, Max. We should do it more often."

"Sounds good."

The smile she gave him ricocheted around inside him like one of those balls in a lottery draw.

"You take care," Max said, anxious to be off and have his reawakened emotions fade back into oblivion. A chief of police didn't need emotions. Just brains and guts.

"I hope I helped." She hesitated as if she wanted to say more, then opened the door and climbed out. One last wave and she was gone. Max started the engine and took a deep breath, ready to feel the relief seep into his mind.

It didn't.

At the end of the driveway he turned left and headed down to headquarters. He didn't know if Bernie was one of the Avenger's victims or not, but four others were. And if he didn't find the guy and get him off the streets soon, there would be a fifth. It was only a matter of time.

BERNIE LEFT THE HOSPITAL Sunday afternoon. He didn't need a specialist to tell him his heart was pumping. Didn't need anyone to tell him that someone had tried to kill him Friday night, either.

Nothing surprising in that. There were lots of people who'd be glad to see him turn up dead. He just hadn't expected them to be attending a society function in Courage Bay. He'd have to start watching his back every minute, no longer just when he was on his L.A. turf.

He grabbed a bottle of water from the fridge and stepped onto his back deck. The view of the Pacific Ocean was breathtaking, worth every penny of the exorbitant price of the house. More than his mother had made in a lifetime of backbreaking work cleaning other women's houses.

She'd even died in one, mopping someone else's dirty floors. The hurt dug into him, felt like a buzzard's claws piercing his heart. He'd thought if he made enough money, if he insinuated himself into the lives of wealthy people like the ones who'd once hired his mother to clean their houses, he'd vindicate her suffering and eradicate the pain.

One day it might, but it hadn't happened yet.

He walked across his yard, stepped out the gate of his security fence and headed toward the edge of the steep precipice. Using his hand to shade his eyes from the sun, he looked down at the churning waves beating against the outcropping of jagged rocks.

A flash of heat and pain hit the back of his head. That was the last thing he was aware of as he toppled over the edge of the cliff and plunged to the rocks below.

CHAPTER THREE

IT WAS A HELL OF A TIME for his chief of detectives to be attending a terrorist training session with the CIA in Washington D.C., Max decided as he drove away from the scene of Courage Bay's latest murder. Not only was Adam Guthrie out of town, but Flint Mauro, his new assistant chief, was still on his honeymoon. Either of them would have been perfect to head up the latest murder investigation.

Who was he kidding? As much as he'd like to have Adam and Flint around to team up with, Max had no intention of taking just a supervisory role with this case. This latest murder might be connected to the Avenger, and that was more than he could stomach.

The Avenger's days were numbered. It was no idle threat. Not even a warning. It was just plain fact.

The TV newsmen were waiting when Max skidded to a stop in his private parking spot at police headquarters. The whole lot were insatiable vultures, but he didn't doubt for a second that he'd be just as persistent were he a newsman instead of a cop. He just never understood how bad news traveled so fast.

The cameras started popping the second he stepped out of his car. Someone stuck a microphone in his face.

"Do you think the latest murder is the work of the serial killer known as the Avenger?"

"There's no conclusive proof of anything at this time."

"Is it true that Bernie Brusco had connections with organized crime?"

Max kept walking. "No comment at this time."

"Will you form a serial killer task force?"

Yeah, and he was it. "Bernie Brusco's murder will be fully investigated using every resource we have."

"Do you think the killer could be a Courage Bay police officer?"

"It could be anyone," Max said. "That's it for now."

"Will you be holding a press conference?"

"Should ordinary citizens be afraid?"

"Do you have suspects?"

The questions kept flying at him as he ducked inside the building, but he waved them off. The reporters would soon fall away, heading back to their newspaper desks and TV stations with the little they knew. A Sunday afternoon murder in the prestigious neighborhood of Jacaranda Heights would be the lead story in all the media. The Avenger would no doubt get a great deal of satisfaction from the attention.

Max dropped to the chair behind his desk, one of the reporters' questions sticking in his mind like a gearshift that wouldn't budge. Did he think the perp could be a cop? Not that the question surprised him. Lawmen were obvious candidates for avenger-type murders. There wasn't a cop out there who at some point didn't get sick and tired of putting his or her life on the line while the legal system passed more and more laws to protect the guilty and the justice system kept releasing the criminals and throwing them back on the streets.

Max knew and trusted his force down to a person. Still, knowing the facts about avenger-type killings made his choice clear. He'd go this investigation alone, and he'd be as objective as was humanly possible when it came to evidence. No one, positively no one, would be off-limits as a suspect if the evidence pointed to them. But he was definitely not buying into the mind set that this had to be a cop.

Avenger-type killings took a certain type of individual, one who could plan and carry out an execution with a sense of purpose and duty. One who accepted the role of judge and jury and had no qualms about issuing a death sentence. Historically these killers weren't cold-hearted or evil the way most murderers were.

They weren't psychopaths, either. If anything, they were usually oversensitive to right and wrong—saw everything in black and white with no shades of gray in the mix. A lot of people with no connection to law enforcement fit that profile.

The sun was setting, and elongated shadows crawled across the room as Max walked into his office and dropped into his chair. He pulled out his notes and started the gruesome task of dissecting every detail that he'd collected at the crime scene. There was very little to go on.

Bernie lived at the highest point of Jacaranda Heights, and had a much steeper drop-off than most of the other residents. Even if the bullet hadn't killed him, the fall would have.

There had been no exit wound, so it was a safe bet that they'd find the bullet somewhere inside the skull. Forensics would be able to narrow down the type of weapon and possibly an estimate of the distance it had traveled before making contact.

Weary now, Max got up and walked over to the file cabinet, where he pulled the four files of the previous murders. He'd go through them one by one, immerse himself in the facts surrounding each case, review them day and night until some pattern emerged.

No murder was perfect. The evidence was always there. The challenge was in finding and recognizing it.

First file, first murder—Hollywood producer Dylan Deeb. The killer obviously found Deeb's sexual exploitation of underage actresses repugnant enough to assign Deeb a death sentence.

Max's cell phone rang. He checked the number on the ID. Callie Baker. He stupidly raked his fingers through his hair as if she could see him, before he cleared his throat and took the call.

"Hello, Callie."

"Max, I was hoping I could catch you."

Her words sizzled along his nerve endings, and he

wondered how a mere voice could produce that sensation. But then it wasn't a mere voice. It was Callie's.

"Is anything wrong?" he asked.

"I just turned on my TV for the evening news. They said Bernie Brusco was murdered."

Damn. He could have let her know since Brusco had been her patient. "I'm sorry, Callie. I should have called you and told you about the murder."

"Then someone did intentionally try to kill him at Mary's party."

"We don't have proof of that."

"But it makes sense. The excessive amounts of ephedra didn't work, so someone shot him and pushed him over the cliff behind his house to damage the evidence."

"You looking to give up medicine and become a detective, Callie?"

"No, I figure I can do both."

She was teasing, but that didn't make her interest in being involved in this case go down any easier. "Didn't we have this conversation at lunch yesterday and decide that you should stay out of the investigation?"

"We did, but that was when Bernie was alive, and attempted murder was only speculation."

The sizzle along his nerve endings cooled to caustic apprehension. "The investigation is police business, Callie. I can't bring you into it any more than you'd have me come in and write prescriptions for your patients or dispense medical advice."

"But you could administer first aid in an emergency if you were on the spot. That's all I'm proposing."

"Define your version of first aid."

"I'll write out a list of everyone I remember seeing at the party Friday night just before or after Bernie collapsed. I know you said it could have been one of the hired staff instead of a guest, but at least this would give you a place to start."

"I can get the guest list from Mary Hancock."

"Sure you can, and I know you will, but that won't narrow down the guests who were still there when Bernie had his attack. I've thought about it, and I can identify a lot of the people who were standing around both before and after I went to Bernie's aid. Besides, if you ask Mary about the whereabouts of guests at specific times, she may feel as if she's incriminating them. It's my guess she'll be hesitant to do that. I, on the other hand, have no qualms about supplying you with information. And I know about Jerry Hawkins."

"Who's Jerry Hawkins?"

"A guest at the party who I have reason to believe is a suspect—and the reason you should talk to me."

Damn. She was speaking his language, and there was no way he could turn down her offer for information. There should be no risk involved with that—not as long as she spoke only to him and didn't let anyone else know that she was giving him the inside scoop.

No risk for her.

Being with Callie was always a risk for him. Tough

to have a heart too stupid to know when it didn't have a chance. Fortunately Max had a brain that did. He was meat and potatoes. Callie was caviar.

Besides, even if they got past that, he was lousy at dating, and his brief dive into the pool of matrimonial bliss had been a disaster. Things got too tangled when he tried to fit his life with someone else's, and he hated tangles that didn't end with an arrest.

His marriage had been years ago, when he was fresh out of college and a rookie on the force. It had lasted all of eight weeks, not even past what most would consider the honeymoon stage. She'd left him, claimed he was married to his job and had no time for a wife. He hadn't fought the breakup since he figured she just might be right.

"We have to talk, Max," Callie insisted.

"Yeah. I could meet with you sometime tomorrow," he said, resigning himself to the fact that he'd have to face this like a man. Then again, that was the problem.

"I have an incredibly full day. What about tomorrow evening? Dinner at my place?"

He swallowed a groan. Dinner at Callie's would mean a half dozen forks laid out like a puzzle, crystal stems that he'd probably knock over and break, and something he'd have to choke down like that raw fish wrapped in seaweed that was so popular these days. Worse, it would mean trying to digest food while his insides did weird things every time she smiled or made eye contact.

"Nothing fancy," she said. "Come as you are."

Sure, with a loaded gun on his hip and another in his trousers that could get him into real trouble. "What time?"

"Sevenish."

"Cops don't have sevenish on their watches. Seven-ten, seven-twenty, seven twenty-two, but not sevenish."

"Seven-ten," she said. "See you then?"

"I'll be there. In the meantime, don't talk to anyone about the fact that you're providing me with information."

"I hadn't planned to spread it around, but surely I can mention it to Mikki?"

"No one. Not even Mikki."

He sat staring at the open file in front of him after he broke the connection. He didn't want to frighten Callie unnecessarily, but the Avenger was getting bolder by the murder. Who knew when he'd cross his own line, decide that his work was so important that it didn't matter who he had to kill to protect himself and his mission? Max planned to make damn sure the threat didn't extend to Callie.

Then as always when Max's thoughts centered on Callie, the old memory started burning inside him. One night, eight long years ago. His breath caught as he remembered the pressure of her breasts pressed against him, the feel of her hot tears on his neck. The sweet, salty taste of her lips.

Now he was having dinner with her at her place. He had to be out of his mind.

IT WAS SURPRISING and somewhat alarming to Callie that she was getting such a high from her sideline involvement in a murder case. Not that she wasn't extremely upset that Bernie had been killed. She was.

But solving a murder case was a whole lot different from puzzling over a medical case.

Both involved life and death and a lot of hypothesis, but the killer in Bernie's case was a calculating human instead of a disease. That changed the game plan considerably. She'd started on her guest list immediately after her conversation with Max last night, and the task had so consumed her that she hadn't fallen asleep until after midnight.

Worse, the case had crept back into her mind between every patient this morning and during the last twenty minutes while Matilda Golena had gone on and on describing every ache and pain she'd felt since the last visit. At eighty-nine, Matilda had lots of aches and pains.

Callie glanced at her watch as Matilda walked out of her office with a clean bill of health in spite of her age and complaints. Twelve twenty-five. If Callie hurried, she could grab a salad from the hospital cafeteria and have another thirty minutes to make notes about people on her list before she met with the head of nurses to discuss new staff requirements in the outpatient surgery center.

She took the elevator down to the cafeteria, chose her salad and was paying for it when she noticed Abby Hawkins sitting by herself at a table a few feet away. Callie felt a surge of adrenaline. She'd promised Max she wouldn't discuss the fact that she was cooperating with him in the murder investigation, but that didn't mean she couldn't talk to friends, even one whose son was at the very top of Callie's list. And if some tidbit of valuable information happened to fall in her lap, that was just good fortune.

"Mind if I join you?" she asked, stopping at Abby's table.

"Please do."

Callie took the food from her tray and set it opposite Abby's. "Did you volunteer in the addiction unit again this morning?"

"Yes. Every Monday and Wednesday. I teach painting classes to the patients who are interested. Some of them are quite talented, but even the ones who aren't seem to benefit from the release of splashing colors on a blank canvas."

"I knew you volunteered. I never realized you taught painting or that you were an artist yourself, for that matter."

"I hadn't painted in years, but started dabbling again after the divorce," Abby said. "I have a few paintings exhibited in Norton's Gallery, but hope to do a show next spring."

"I'm impressed. I'll have to drop by Norton's."

"Don't expect too much. My talent is minimal."

"Jack Norton must not think so. Did Elizabeth and Jerry inherit your talent?"

Abby's eyebrows rose. "Oh, so you met Jerry?"

"Yes. I ran into him as he was leaving Mary Hancock's party Friday night and he introduced himself. I didn't know you had a son."

"He doesn't visit often, but he's off work recuperating from an injury, so he's spending a couple of weeks with me."

Whatever his injury was, it hadn't been obvious at the party. "Where does he live?"

"Sacramento."

"If he needs follow-up care while he's here, perhaps I could see him or suggest another physician."

"He's fine," Abby answered between bites of her sandwich. "Bored, but fine. That's the only reason he went to Mary's party the other night. He normally avoids anything that requires more formal attire than jeans or shorts. But he loves to go boating, and I've agreed to go with him this afternoon, so I better run."

Too bad. Callie would love to hear more, especially how a man from Sacramento knew so much about Bernie Brusco.

More info to share with Max tonight—which brought to mind a few other problems. Like why having an old friend to dinner to discuss a police investigation incited titillating sensations at the edge of her consciousness.

But then she'd never understood her feelings for Max Zirinsky, not since that night she'd boo-hooed in his arms over his pompous, self-centered cousin, whom she'd had the poor judgment to marry.

She was ready to trash what was left of her salad and get back to her office when she heard Mikki's laughter over the clatter of banging trays and chatter. Mikki spotted her at the same time, smiled and came hurrying over with a heaping plate of spaghetti and meatballs and a slice of coconut pie.

"Are you expecting a crowd for lunch?" Callie asked as Mikki started unloading her tray.

"I hope not. I plan to eat every bite of this myself. I missed my midmorning apple and I'm famished."

"Busy morning?"

"Swimmer's ear. I think half the population of Courage Bay under fifteen years of age is water-logged. The rest are sunburned or else they're faking stomachaches so they don't have to leave their friends and go to summer camp."

Mikki forked a tangled mass of dangling spaghetti and slid it between her lips.

"And wasn't that man who was murdered last night the same guy you saw in the emergency room Friday night?" she asked as soon as she'd swallowed.

"One and the same."

"Did you see the headlines in the morning paper?"

"No."

"Another one bites the dust. They devoted half a page to talking about the Avenger. They make this killer sound like a cross between Superman and the Terminator."

"You know how the media loves hype," Callie said.

"Hype's one thing. Glorifying a killer is another. What if we all went around killing everyone we wanted dead?" She broke off a bite of her bread and slathered it with butter. "And I caught a bit of the noon news. They showed your friend Max. He's more than just a nice butt, you know. You really should go after him."

"Go after him?"

"Yeah, you know, flaunt your stuff the way you did in that red dress Friday night. The poor guy was practically drooling."

"I didn't notice his tongue hanging out."

"Tongues can be tricky. Sometimes you have to go in after them."

"That's as gross as watching you sit here in your size four pants and shovel down what amounts to a month's calories for the rest of us."

"Someone has to eat this hospital food. But speaking of calories, your favorite resident at the Keller Center is putting on too many pounds again."

"You must be speaking of Gail Lodestrum."

"None other than our emotional wreck who's carrying not one but two fetuses in her womb.

"Did you go up this weekend?"

"Yesterday. Cortina delivered, and I couldn't wait a whole week to see the new baby."

"Boy or girl?"

"A dark-haired boy. Perfectly healthy, and totally adorable."

"Great. Not good news about Gail, though."

"No. I tried to talk to her, but she shut me out like always, except to ask when you'd be back. For some reason, you seem to be the only one she trusts."

"She's only fifteen," Callie said. "I probably remind her of her mother."

"The mother who kicked her out of the house when she found out Gail was pregnant. I seriously doubt it. When are the twins due?"

"Early September, but I think they'll come early," Callie said, pushing her salad plate out of the way and propping her elbows on the table. "She clams up every time I ask her about the father, but I have a feeling she hasn't told him about the babies. If she did, she might get a little support there. Or maybe not."

"She'll tell you all before it's over. They always bare their souls to you, even when they won't talk to the counselors at the center."

"Pregnant women and dogs like me."

"And police chiefs."

Callie felt a slow burn that she was certain reached her cheeks. One of the surgery residents stopped by the table to hit on Mikki before Callie had time to respond. "Great timing," she told him without bothering to explain what she meant. She said a quick goodbye and headed back to her office.

She was sure Mikki was wrong about Max. If he was attracted to her, she'd be the first to know.

Wouldn't she?

UNLOCKING AND OPENING the door, Callie stepped inside the rambling beach house she'd inherited from her aunt Louise. Late afternoon sunshine poured through the windows, adding a golden glow to the cream-colored walls, honeyed pine furniture and vivid colors of the up-holstered pieces. Pickering got up lazily from his spot in front of the back door and came to greet her.

"Hello, boy. Did you miss me?"

He licked her hand in answer.

Callie slipped out of her shoes and left them at the door, loving the feel of the polished wood against her bare feet as she padded to the kitchen to drop off the white deli bags that held tonight's dinner. Finger foods that she and Max could eat around the pool as the sun settled to a ball of fire and dropped into the Pacific.

Taking a minute, Callie rummaged through the day's mail, which she'd picked up on her way in. A few advertising circulars, a couple of catalogs, and an engraved invitation to a wedding reception. Which reminded her of another engagement. The Cravens' annual garden party was Saturday afternoon. She'd have to remember to call her regrets tomorrow.

Though the party would be nice—social affairs in Marjorie Craven's beautiful English garden always were—Callie wanted to drive up to the center on Saturday and have a talk with Gail. Keeping the mother of twins healthy took precedence over tea and scones.

Callie's thoughts drifted back to Max as she chose an assortment of wine and arranged the food on serving plates. The last time he'd been to this house had been a rainy night eight years ago, just three weeks after she and Tony had moved in. Looking back, she'd never been sure why Max had stopped by that night. He'd never done it before or since.

The room grew warm as the memories rushed in. Okay, if she kept this up, she was likely to hurl herself into Max's arms again and he'd run off for another eight years.

It was only six-forty. If she hurried, she'd have time for a quick swim before he arrived. That should cool her off.

She slipped into a black bathing suit and was about to dive into the pool when her cell phone rang. The caller ID said Mary Hancock. The swim could wait a few more minutes.

"Hi, Mary."

"I was visiting a friend in San Diego today, and I just heard about Bernie," Mary said, her voice hoarse and broken. "The newscaster said he'd been murdered."

"I'm sorry, Mary. I had no idea you didn't know or I would have called you earlier."

"They're saying the Avenger killed him."

"That's speculation."

"Not according to the news. The Avenger made a mistake. Bernie wasn't involved in drugs. That was just a story concocted by his enemies. He explained it all to me."

"I know it's hard to believe something bad about friends, especially…"

"We were more than friends."

Callie's spirits sank. "How much more?"

"He'd asked me to marry him. I was thinking about saying yes."

Marriage. That did come as a surprise, and not only

because of the age difference. "How long have you known him?"

"Only about three months, but he was so thoughtful. And we had fun together."

"You certainly seemed to."

"Bernie's collapse at my party may not have been an accident, Callie. Whoever shot him yesterday may have tried to kill him at my party."

"I suppose that's possible." No reason to lie about that.

"I may have invited this Avenger person into my home."

"You didn't do it knowingly."

"No, but it makes me sick to think he could be one of us. I plan to find out for sure."

"I don't think you should try to handle this yourself, Mary. Just cooperate with the police."

"I'll cooperate, all right. I don't want Bernie's killer going free."

By the time she got off the phone with Mary, Callie really needed a swim. She dove in and tried to drive the images of murder from her mind with vigorous breast strokes. Instead, the troublesome thoughts merged and mingled with the old memories. Murder, mayhem and Max—a sure recipe for disaster.

The doorbell rang as she pulled herself from the pool. Her guest had arrived.

CHAPTER FOUR

MAX RANG CALLIE'S DOORBELL at exactly seven-ten. At seven-eleven, his heart was in his throat. Callie had said come as you are, but he hadn't expected her to be quite this informal.

Water dripped from her hair onto her shoulders, and the black bathing suit hugged her tiny waist and accentuated her perky breasts. Max inhaled sharply and averted his gaze. "Am I early?"

"No. I took a quick swim, but it will only take me a few minutes to slip into something else," she explained, drying the ends of her hair with a fluffy red beach towel. She led him into the kitchen, where a large golden retriever was lapping water from a green doggy bowl.

"This is Pickering," she said, stooping to give the dog a few reassuring pats. "He rules the house."

"Nice pad you got here, Pickering," Max said, putting out his hand for the retriever to sniff.

"I put out a few choices for wine," Callie said. "Why don't you pick out one and open it while I change?"

"I can handle that."

Once it was only him and Pickering in the kitchen,

Max breathed a little easier. It was crazy to let Callie get to him like this, but she always had, and there was no reason to think tonight would be any different. He was tough. He'd handle it, as long as what she changed into covered more than the skimpy bathing suit had.

Concentrating on the wine, Max considered his choices. He was a beer man himself, but he selected a California Merlot, uncorked the bottle and poured the wine into the crystal decanter Callie had left on the counter. That done, he walked through the open back door and onto the deck with Pickering at his heels. The view was magnificent, an expanse of beach bordered by frothy waves lapping onto the sand.

The house was in an exclusive part of Courage Bay, expensive as all waterfront property was, but not as isolated or protected as Bernie Brusco's home in Jacaranda Heights. There was no steep, rocky hillside leading up from the water's edge, no natural barriers to keep someone on the beach from walking right up to the black privacy fence that separated Callie's pool and house from the rest of the beach.

Thinking like a cop, he reminded himself. The truth was, this area was privately patrolled and had one of the lowest crime rates in the county.

He turned at the sound of footsteps behind him. One look at Callie and thoughts of crime and safety flew out of his mind. He was back to square one, turned on to the point that all he could do was stare.

Her tanned, shapely legs looked even longer in a pair

of white shorts. Her yellow shirt was open at the neck and her reddish-brown hair curved about her naturally blushed cheeks.

No woman should look that good.

"Are you starved?" she asked.

Famished, but not for food. "Not particularly."

"How about a walk along the beach before we get down to business? A walk always helps me relax and clear my mind after a hectic day at the hospital."

He hesitated, pretty sure that a sunset walk with Callie wasn't going to do a thing toward clearing his mind or keeping his libido in check. But she had an expectant look in her eyes and he'd sound like a jerk if he said no.

"A walk sounds good," he lied. There he was in his chinos, pulled right from the rack of the local department store, while Callie wore a pair of white shorts that fit so perfectly they looked as if they'd been tailor-made. Even her toenails were dressed for the occasion, painted red in a finish that made them look wet and shiny.

It struck him once again as he slipped out of his brown leather loafers and cotton socks that his cousin Tony was an absolute fool.

THE COOL, SALTY BREEZE tossed Callie's hair and she skipped through the surf for a few yards like a kid on summer vacation. Seeing her like this, Max found it difficult to imagine that she was a physician, much less chief of staff of a hospital the size of Courage Bay. She picked up a stick and threw it, and Pickering ran off to fetch it.

A few minutes later, she settled into an easy gait beside Max while Pickering raced ahead, stopping every so often to make sure his mistress was still behind him.

"I've been thinking about Bernie's murder all day," she confessed. "I'm beginning to see how detectives get so caught up in their cases. The Avenger case must have cost you a few sleepless nights."

"More than a few," he admitted.

"The news report said that at least four revenge-type murders can be tied to one killer. Is that accurate?"

"The link is all speculation, but probably accurate. There was Dylan Deeb back in November."

"I remember that," Callie said. "Strangled, wasn't he, and left to go down with his house in the mud slide?"

"Right. Then in January, you alerted me to the suspicious bruises on Bruce Nepom."

"No way to forget that one. A roofing scam artist bludgeoned to death just before his own roof collapsed on him during the storm of the century."

"Another guy guilty of murder who walked," Max said. "His defective materials killed the Mahoneys as surely as if he'd shot them with a pistol. We all knew Nepom was guilty. We just couldn't get the evidence on him."

"I wondered if one of the Mahoneys' grown kids might have killed Nepom," Callie said.

"None of their children were even in the state when Nepom died. And while we've found plenty of people he scammed who admit to being glad he's dead, none of them checked out as viable suspects in his death."

Pickering darted into the surf, then out again, spraying them with water.

"Who's the third victim?" Callie asked, finding another stick that had washed up on the beach and tossing it for Pickering.

"Lorna Sinke."

"She died in the hospital after being shot in the hostage situation at City Hall."

"The bullet didn't come from the hostage takers' guns, nor from the SWAT team. The weapon that fired the fatal shot was never located."

"Then doesn't that narrow down your suspects considerably?"

"It does, if in fact Lorna was killed by the Avenger. But there's always the possibility that Lorna was shot by someone who wanted her dead for reasons other than her suspected guilt in her parents' murder, someone who just took advantage of the situation and thought the death would be blamed on crossfire between the police and the hostage takers."

"She was a little strange," Callie admitted, "and she worked at City Hall as an aide to council, so she had ample opportunity to make enemies there." Callie stooped to examine a large shell that had washed onto the beach, then resumed walking at her same brisk pace. "Do you think Lorna was actually guilty of shoving her parents down the stairs?"

"Evidence indicated she gave them a drug that made them so disoriented they fell to their death on their own."

"But she walked," Callie said. "Makes you wonder how many guilty people get off scot-free."

"Won't need a scorecard to keep that record in Courage Bay if the Avenger keeps killing them off. The guilty will soon start begging for prison terms just to stay alive."

"That leaves Carlos Esposito," Callie said. "I can almost understand why the Avenger killed that guy. When I heard how he stole children from their parents in Mexico and brought them into the States as migrant workers, I wanted to kill him myself."

"But you didn't."

"Of course not."

"Which is what sets the Avenger apart from the rest of us."

"What did cause the plane crash that killed him?"

"The plane's engine had been tampered with."

Callie slowed, and something hard and determined crept into her voice. "We have to stop him, Max, or he'll just keep killing, and someday he'll kill an innocent person."

Max took her arm and tugged her to a stop. "*We* don't have to stop him, Callie. I agreed to talk to you about the case tonight. That's all. You're not putting yourself in the middle of a murder investigation."

"Technically the Avenger dragged me into it when he slipped the ephedra overdose into Bernie's food right under my nose," Callie said. "Now I'm just acting as any concerned citizen."

"There were lots of citizens at Mary Hancock's party the other night. None of the others are involved in the investigation."

"I know, but I feel responsible somehow. After all, I released Bernie from the hospital and he walked straight into the path of a bullet."

"Get that thought out of your mind. No one's responsible for the murder except the killer."

She hugged her arms about her chest. "Still, if I can help, I want to. Why don't we go back to the house," she said, "and get down to dinner and business?"

He nodded, but when their eyes met, a bewildering sensation skidded along his nerve endings. It had been a mistake to let Callie become even this involved in the investigation. And now he had to wonder if it hadn't been his desire to see her again that had caused him to agree to have dinner with her tonight.

If so, he'd really stepped over the line. Police work and romance didn't mix. Hell, romance and anything had never mixed too well in his life. Most of all, he would not pull her into any kind of danger. And the Avenger was a very dangerous man—or woman.

THEY ATE AT A SMALL table by the pool, and fortunately Max didn't have to juggle the forks. There were none. The meal was simple, but good. Crusty bread, several kinds of cheese and deli meats, pickles, deviled eggs and fruit, all accompanied by a fruity wine.

They talked very little until the meal was finished.

Max stretched out and stared at the disappearing sun. "Great view."

"Isn't it? I love living on the water. What about you, Max? You surely aren't still in that same tiny apartment you were in when I was married to Tony?"

"Same place, but I don't do much more than sleep there."

She tilted her head and arched her brows. "You must have a pretty hot social life."

"Super hot. You saw it firsthand Friday night. All alone at the bar."

"You should take up a hobby or at least get away once in a while."

"I do every now and then. Tony and I and a couple of his doctor pals from Los Angeles did some fishing in Mexico last summer—just before the heat wave hit Courage Bay." Max swallowed hard, afraid after the fact that the mention of Tony might upset Callie, but if it did, she showed no signs.

Callie sipped her wine. "How is Tony?"

"Same old, same old. On his third wife. No kids. Still rather play than work and complains all the time because he doesn't make the kind of money he thought he would as a doctor."

"You're right. Same old, same old."

Callie excused herself, then returned a minute later with a legal pad and a pen. "I've been thinking about what you said on the beach about Lorna Sinke. At least two of the people still at the party Friday night when

Bernie collapsed were in the room with the hostages at City Hall when Lorna was killed."

"D.A. Lalane?"

"He's one. I know Henry was still there, because I had just been talking to him."

Max nodded. She'd hit that squarely on the head.

"Judge Craven was still there as well," Callie told him.

"He and Henry were both on the scene when Lorna was shot," Max admitted. "But tell me about this Jerry Hawkins that you mentioned."

Callie toyed with her wineglass, letting her perfectly manicured nails travel up and down the stem. "I met him when we were both getting our cars to leave the party. He informed me that Bernie Brusco made his money distributing drugs in the Los Angeles area and that I should have let him die."

"So that's how you knew about Bernie's background. What else do you know about Jerry Hawkins?"

"His mother is Abby Hawkins. She lives in the old section of Paramont Estates. I know her from the hospital. She volunteers a couple of days a week, but I also run into her frequently at fund-raisers and parties. She never mentioned having a son."

"I take it she has money."

"She divorced well."

Max listened to Callie's concerns that Jerry had seemed bored and disinterested at the party, and had to agree that the guy did warrant being checked out. But Max doubted he was the Avenger. For one thing, he lived in Sacramento, and Max had a strong hunch that even if the Avenger hadn't been in City Hall the day of the hostage situation, he probably still lived here in Courage Bay. This type of killer usually had strong ties to the community where he operated.

Callie went through a dozen more names, people she knew who were in the area when Bernie collapsed. If Max had been on the scene himself, he doubted he could have done better.

When she finished her spiel, she reached beneath the table and gave Pickering's ears a good scratch. She stretched her feet beneath the table and her bare toes brushed his. The touch set off pangs of awareness that settled painfully in his groin.

Murder and lust. Suspects and wine. Business and Callie in a pair of shorts that hit high on her thighs.

"I think it's time we call it a night," he said, willing the stirring of arousal to settle down so that it wasn't obvious when he stood.

"I do have an early day tomorrow," she said.

He thanked her for dinner again as she walked him to the door. The moment was awkward. Extending his hand seemed too formal. A kiss seemed too... Too damn tempting.

But Callie didn't leave the decision to him. She leaned in close and pressed her lips to his cheek. He lifted his arms to put them around her, then let them drop back to his side.

"I'm glad you came," Callie murmured, pulling away again.

"Yeah. Thanks for dinner and the info. See you." Max knew he sounded and looked like a green high school kid. He quickly turned and left Callie standing in the doorway.

The quiet surf seemed like thunder roaring in his ears as he climbed behind the wheel of his car. He could face murderers, snipers, the worst crud of the street and never have them see him sweat. But let Callie Baker give him a peck on the cheek and he fell apart faster than a $3.99 T-shirt from the hawker at the beach.

Wouldn't the Avenger love to see him now?

CALLIE STOOD at the front door and watched Max back down the driveway, turn his car on a dime and squeal his tires in his haste to escape. It had been the same eight years ago, almost as if he was afraid of her.

She dropped to the sofa and let the memories claim her mind. She'd been angry and hurt that night, totally disillusioned to find that while she'd been desperately trying to hold on to her crumbling marriage, Tony had been having an affair behind her back.

She'd ordered him out of the house and out of her life—and accompanied that command with a hurled wineglass that had missed his temple by inches. It was probably the first and last time she'd thrown anything at anyone. Then she'd collapsed on the sofa and burst into tears.

When the doorbell rang a few minutes later, she was certain it was Tony, back with more lies. But when she'd opened the door, Max was standing there. As best she could remember, neither of them said a word. She'd just stepped into his arms and held on tight. For the life of her, she couldn't remember how they went from there to a kiss.

But she did remember that kiss. Wow, did she remember that kiss. It was as if every pent-up emotion she'd ever felt erupted in a blast of passion.

There was no denying Max had felt something, too. His arousal had pressed into her and his mouth had ravished hers until her lips were swollen from the force of that kiss. A heated blush crept over her skin and her insides turned to mush just thinking about it.

But she was forty now, not thirty-two. A respected and formidable hospital chief of staff, not a woman faced with the fact that she'd married a self-serving louse. If the moment of passion she'd shared with Max was no more than a reaction to her emotional state all those years ago, then it was time to move past it.

But if there was still some kind of spark waiting to catch fire, it was time to find that out, too. Of course, she might have to tie Max down to do it.

"DO YOU THINK I'm intimidating?" Callie asked as she poured herself a cup of flavored coffee from the pot in Mikki's office.

Mikki stopped nibbling on a cookie, her second since she'd finished the sandwich and banana she'd had for lunch. "No more so than a five-star general in battle mode."

"I'm not talking about at work, but on a personal level."

"You scare the hell out of me and I've seen you scooping up Pickering's poop." Mikki dumped the crumbs from her napkin into the trash can by her desk. "What makes you ask?"

"No reason."

"You never say or do anything for no reason, Callie, which only ups your intimidation factor."

"I just wonder if I throw off some kind of vibes that frighten men off."

"No more than any other beautiful, highly successful, nearly perfect woman would."

"Be serious."

"I am."

"So how would I change that conception of me?" Callie asked. "That is, if I wanted to change it?"

"For starters, you could be a little less self-sufficient. Men love to feel needed, makes them feel like hunky heroes. But to be honest with you, I can't see Max Zirinsky being intimidated by anyone."

Callie's right hand flew to her hip. "Who said this discussion has anything to do with Max Zirinsky?"

"Boy, hit that exposed nerve, didn't I?" Mikki teased.

Callie started to argue, but knew it was a waste of time. Mikki read her too well. Besides, the one night Max had let down his guard with her had been the night he'd found her in tears, so maybe Mikki did know a thing or two about men. Still, Callie had no intention of tearing up just to make the guy feel needed.

She sipped her coffee. "I'm not playing 'poor little defenseless me' for anybody."

"Good. You could never pull that off. I'm thinking more in the line of requesting back rubs for tense muscles or asking for help with leaky faucets or quirky zippers—especially help with quirky zippers."

"That sounds like manipulation to me. Besides, I don't have any quirky zippers." She glanced at her watch, then gulped down the rest of her coffee. "Okay, girlfriend, gotta run. I have a full slate of patients this afternoon."

"Me, too. But then I always do. Apparently birth control hasn't caught on in Courage Bay."

There were three patients in Callie's waiting room when she got back to her office. Max and quirky zippers were pushed to the back of her mind as she went to work on the problems at hand.

First and foremost, she was a doctor.

"You have a call from Mary Hancock. She says it's urgent."

Callie paused, her hand on the doorknob to examining room three. "Did she say what kind of emergency?"

Her nurse shook her head. "I asked, but all she said was that she needed to talk to you at once."

"I'll take the call in my office."

"It's line one."

Callie hurried to her office and grabbed the receiver. "What's wrong, Mary?"

"It's about Bernie."

Callie's muscles relaxed. She didn't have time for this right now, but it was better than chest pains or signs of a stroke, always the first things that popped into her mind when someone said emergency. "What about Bernie?"

"I think I know who killed him, Callie."

That piqued her interest. "Who?"

"I don't want to say until I have a little more evidence, but if it's who I think it is, you're going to be shocked. Everyone in Courage Bay is going to be shocked."

"If you have any information, you need to call Max Zirinsky at the police department."

"No, I don't want to get mixed up with the police, at least not yet. But I need to talk to someone. I was hoping you could stop by when you leave the hospital tonight."

"That won't be for another couple of hours. I still have patients to see and hospital rounds to make."

"That will be perfect. The caterer has tracked down another of the servers for me to question. She's on her way over here now."

"Do you think it was one of the catering staff who killed Bernie?"

"No, but they were in a position to see things that none of the rest of us saw, like someone slipping a powder into Bernie's drink. I just need someone to add credence to my theory."

The conversation was making Callie exceedingly uneasy. "I don't think you should talk to anyone else about this, Mary."

"I don't, either. That's why I called you. If you think my suspicions are accurate, then I'll go to the police. It's just if I'm right, the killer is…"

"Is what?"

"A very close relative of a dear friend, and I can't say more now, Callie. I never trust these cell phones. I've read that people can overhear your conversation without your ever knowing it."

"I'll be there as quickly as I can."

"Thanks, Callie." Mary gave her the code to get in the security gate before saying goodbye.

Callie broke the connection but hung on to the receiver, wondering if she should call and alert Max. If she did, he'd act on the tip immediately and Mary would feel betrayed. Probably better to call him from Mary's so she could be there when Max came out to question her friend.

It wasn't likely that the Avenger had been so careless as to let the catering staff see him slip the ephedra into Bernie's food or drink. Yet stupider things had happened.

A close relative of a dear friend. That could be half of Courage Bay. Everyone was Mary's friend. And if the Avenger turned out to be someone in attendance at Mary's party, a lot of people would be shocked.

Callie tried to throw off thoughts of the murder as she went into the examining room of her next patient, but she couldn't shake the prickles of dread Mary's tone had caused. She'd have to persuade Mary to talk to Max tonight. He'd convince her that investigating her theory on her own was far too dangerous.

CALLIE RANG THE DOORBELL for the third time. Mary wouldn't have gone out without calling and cancelling their appointment. She had to be around here somewhere. Callie waited a few more minutes, then decided to walk to the back of the house. Maybe Mary was in the garden or the pool.

"Mary." Callie called her friend's name. When there was no response, Callie peeked over the black decorative fence that surrounded the pool. The patio table held two place settings, a small vase of roses and a bottle of wine. So like Mary to have prepared dinner for the two of them.

Callie tried the gate. It wasn't locked, so she let herself in. She'd started toward the French doors off the patio when she caught sight of an overturned lounge chair near the edge of the pool. She walked over to right it, and that's when she spotted Mary. Facedown. Lying on the bottom of the pool at the shallow end.

Callie felt a scream at the back of her throat but couldn't release it. And then she heard the gate squeak open again and knew she was not alone.

CHAPTER FIVE

FRANTIC, CALLIE dropped her handbag, kicked off her shoes and waded into the pool without so much as turning to see who'd joined her. She grabbed the floating arm and tugged Mary to the surface, knowing even before her fingers closed around the lifeless wrist that there would be no pulse.

Still, fighting off waves of shock, she dragged Mary onto the deck and began CPR.

"Oh, my God! What happened? Is she…"

Callie ignored the ragged male voice and did her best to breathe life back into Mary's lungs. She worked until she was forced to face the fact that her revival attempts were useless. When she finally looked up, Henry Lalane was standing over her, his eyes wide and his hands tearing at the silk tie knotted around his neck.

Henry squatted next to Callie and stared at the body. "She's…dead."

Callie nodded, barely aware that water had soaked the bottom half of her slacks and was dripping onto her feet. That her blouse had pulled loose at the waist, and the heat of the late afternoon sun was relentlessly bearing down on her back.

"How?" Henry asked, looking at her as if she should have answers. Why?"

Callie shook her head. "I don't know."

"She was an excellent swimmer," Henry said. "She wouldn't have drowned in her own pool."

"But she did."

"Then she must have had a stroke or a heart attack." He stood and shoved his hands deep in his pockets. His mouth twisted into a scowl. "Or maybe she intentionally drowned herself over that worthless Bernie Brusco."

"No, she wouldn't," Callie protested. "Mary was too level-headed for that."

"I wouldn't be so sure. Anyway, we have to call the cops."

"Right." Callie got up and walked over to her handbag. Retrieving her cell phone, she punched in Max's number. He answered on the second ring.

"Max Zirinsky."

"Max, this is Callie. I'm at Mary Hancock's and…" She took a deep breath and tried to compose her tangled thoughts and get a handle on her emotions. "I found Mary at the bottom of her pool. I pulled her out and tried to revive her, but… She's dead, Max."

Callie could hear the sharp inhalation of Max's breath before he spoke. "Are you okay?"

"Yes."

"Are you sure?"

"I'm shaken, but other than that, I'm fine. Henry Lalane's here with me."

"What's he doing there?"

"I don't know. He just showed up right after I did."

"Then he wasn't there when you arrived."

"No."

"I'll be right over. Don't touch Mary again or anything else. And tell Lalane not to touch anything, either. But I do want him to stay at the scene."

"I'll tell him."

"I'm on my way."

She broke the connection and took a deep breath, trying to regain her professional edge. She turned to Henry, who had walked over to join her. "That was Max Zirinsky. He's on his way."

"Good. So why are you here, anyway?" Henry asked. "Did Mary call and insist you come by, the way she did with me?"

"She asked me to stop by."

"But didn't say why, I guess. You can think what you want, but somehow her relationship with Bernie Brusco is behind this." Henry sank onto the edge of a deck chair. "Mary called me at least a half dozen times today—wanted me to tell her that Bernie was not a piece of drug trafficking scum."

"She was fond of him."

"That was evident." He glanced back toward Mary's lifeless form, but looked away quickly. "I know we can't help her, but shouldn't we at least take her inside or something. I mean, she looks so…" He threw his hands up in frustration. "She looks so dead."

"Max said not to touch Mary or anything else."

"See? He thinks there's something suspicious going on here, too."

"He didn't say that."

"Why else would he be treating this like a crime scene?"

"I don't know. But I'm sure Mary didn't kill herself. She was upset, but not depressed or suicidal. If anything, I'd say she was driven to find Bernie's killer."

Callie walked over and knelt beside Mary again, and this time she noticed small bruises on the flesh at her neck. She shuddered, suddenly overcome with a premonition that something dark and ominous was hovering over them, and it wasn't going to go away anytime soon.

MARY MCGUIRE HANCOCK had been murdered. That was evident almost from the moment the crime scene investigators arrived. The bruises on her neck indicated strangling, probably by a smooth length of fabric, possibly a scarf—or a tie like the one hanging loosely from Henry Lalane's neck.

Max walked away from the CSI team and rejoined Henry Lalane and Callie inside the kitchen of Mary's house. He'd taken both their statements when he'd arrived, but he wanted to talk to them a bit more. Callie wasn't a suspect, but Henry was, especially since he'd been one of the people present in the room when Lorna

Sinke was shot. But no police officer made an accusation of murder against a prestigious and popular district attorney without firm evidence to back it up.

Henry stood when Max walked into the room. "Was it suicide?"

"Preliminary findings indicate strangulation before water entered her lungs. We'll know more after the autopsy report."

"Another senseless killing," Henry railed. "Definitely not the Avenger this time, though. Mary was no criminal."

"No motive has been established," Max said, studying Henry's body language. He could tell almost as much by a man's muscle reactions, facial expressions and eye movements as what he said.

"Any reason you need Callie and me to hang around?" Henry asked.

"If not," Callie added tentatively, "I should get back to the hospital. I need to meet with the relatives of a critical patient in the ICU."

"You can go, Callie," Max said, walking over to look at the latch on the kitchen window while he talked. "I have a few more questions for you, but I can catch you later."

"Thanks."

"No reason for me to stay, either," Henry said. "I've told you everything I know."

"I appreciate that," Max told the district attorney, "but I need to clarify a few things in my own mind."

Henry frowned. "I hope this won't take long. Janice and I have plans tonight."

A little callous, Max thought, considering it was Henry's friend who'd been murdered, but then being questioned by the chief of police at a murder scene would put a lot of people off, especially a very astute district attorney.

"A few minutes should do it," Max assured him, then waited until Callie had said her goodbyes and left. Max would have liked to walk her to her car and tell her how sorry he was she'd had to find Mary like this, but under the circumstances, it would have been awkward for both of them.

He pulled his small black notebook and a pen from inside his jacket pocket. "I know you've already told me about getting a phone call from Mary, but it would help if you'd explain that in detail again."

"Not much to explain. Mary called my office a few minutes before five o'clock. She told my secretary it was urgent, and Doris pulled me out of a meeting with one of my attorneys to talk to her."

"Be as specific as possible. What were the first words Mary said when she got you on the phone?"

"I can't remember exactly, but basically it was 'It's really important that I see you immediately, Henry.' I tried to get her to elaborate, but she refused. Said she didn't want to talk about it over the phone."

"Did she mention Bernie Brusco at all?"

"Not during that phone call, but she'd called me five

or six times earlier in the day. Mostly she asked questions about what I knew about Bernie, but I got the idea she just wanted me to tell her the stories that appeared in the paper about Bernie's being involved in drugs were erroneous. Of course, I couldn't do that. Everything I've heard indicates that he was a major player."

"Did you tell her that?"

"I didn't see any reason to lie."

"Did she sound as if she was afraid or hysterical the last time you talked to her?"

"No, nothing that extreme. She was upset, but no more so than she'd been during the other calls."

"So why did you stop what you were doing and come over here after that last phone call and not the others?"

"Like I said, she insisted that she had to see me at once, and since it was late in the day, I just knocked off and came on over. It never crossed my mind she was in danger."

"Were you a close friend of Mary's?"

"Not at all. Actually, Janice knows her a lot better than I do, but Mary did back my campaign."

That would explain why Henry rushed over at her request, but it didn't explain why Mary had wanted him here. "Strange that she'd make an urgent call to you instead of, say, a close friend," Max observed.

Henry tugged on his already loose tie. "No stranger than calling me all day about Bernie Brusco. The weird thing is that she'd get mixed up with a man like him in the first place—or that he'd get mixed up with her."

"Were you here Friday night when Bernie collapsed?"

Henry hesitated, immediately arousing Max's suspicions.

"I was here. So were several dozen others."

A fact that Max was all too aware of. He asked a few more questions, then thanked Henry and told him he'd get back to him later if he thought of anything else.

"Call me anytime, Max, but I've told you all I know. Keep me posted, though. Find Mary's killer and I'll prosecute him. Any man who'd kill a woman like that should definitely pay."

Max stood at the kitchen window and watched Henry round the pool and go out the back gate. Lalane was known as a highly effective district attorney, as tough on crime as a person could be. Not the type you'd ordinarily think of as a serial murder suspect, but these were not ordinary murders.

And Henry had lost a daughter in a random shooting. Since then, both he and his wife had become outspoken advocates for getting guns off the street. Some people considered Henry a radical on the subject. So he had motive and opportunity—neither of which proved a damn thing.

Max rejoined his CSI team around the pool. Once they'd combed every inch of ground out there, they'd start on the house, but Max's guess from his preliminary observations was that they would find no sign of forced entry. Whoever killed Mary was likely a friend.

If this was the work of the Avenger, the threat the

killer posed had moved up to the next level. He'd crossed the line between targeting the guilty to killing the innocent. Perhaps he'd even crossed the thin line that separated sanity from madness.

Which meant the murders could accelerate at an alarming rate, and no one who crossed the Avenger or got in his way would be safe. Courage Bay would be on high alert.

"THAT HAD TO BE HORRIBLE for you," Mikki said. "Just walking up and finding the body in the pool like that."

"It's not something I'll forget anytime soon," Callie admitted.

"I'm sure. Do you need company? I can be there in under a half hour."

"Thanks for the offer, but actually, Max Zirinsky is on his way over."

"Ooh. Better comfort than I can offer."

"I don't think comfort is part of his agenda. He wants to ask more questions."

"Agendas can be modified."

"You're right. He could decide to arrest me."

"Not a chance. Anyway, you take care, and remember, I'm available if you need me. All you have to do is call."

"Thanks. I appreciate that." Callie hung up the phone and walked out to the back deck. "No walk tonight, Pickering," she said, patting him on the back of the head. She could use the walk to settle her rattled nerves, but Max was due any minute.

She stared at the sunset. Beautiful as it was, it brought no feelings of peacefulness tonight.

Restless, she walked back inside, scanned the day's mail, then reached for the Cravens' invitation. She'd left it out to remind her to call in her regrets since she wanted to visit the Keller Center that day.

She wondered if the Avenger had received an invitation to the garden party. The Avenger could be anyone, anyone at all. A madman in their midst. Even as Callie dropped the invitation into her pocket, a plan was forming in her mind—one Max Zirinsky would likely not agree to without a fight.

IT HAD BEEN AFTER EIGHT when Max arrived at Callie's, later than he'd intended, but he'd stayed at Mary Hancock's with the CSI team until they'd completely finished. He liked to be thorough in his investigations, and evidence seemed to stick in his mind a lot better if he saw it for himself instead of merely reading a report.

He'd finished his second round of questioning Callie in twenty minutes, and now he was lingering, thinking that coming to her house had been a mistake. Sitting on the deck with the backdrop of the breaking surf stole his edge and made him susceptible to his own weaknesses—weaknesses that came into play whenever Callie was involved.

The breeze was gentle and warm and it tousled Callie's hair as if it were strands of silk. She pushed an errant lock behind her right ear, then flicked away a flying insect that had landed on the arm of her deck chair. "Were you able to track down the person from the catering staff who was on her way to see Mary when I talked to her last?" she asked.

"Just by phone. She never made it to Mary's."

"What stopped her?"

"Nothing. She said Mary kept insisting, so the woman just told her she was coming over to get Mary off her back. Mary wanted the server to look at pictures and point out guests who might have wandered into the kitchen during the party."

"She could still do that."

"She could, but she claims people were in and out all night, and she didn't pay enough attention to any of them to give reliable feedback." Max moved his feet to accommodate Pickering, who'd decided to sleep by Max's chair for a while. "I talked to the director of catering, and he said Mary had called them four times today, demanding to talk to various wait staff. I've asked him to assemble the full staff that was at Mary's that night. I'll question them as a group and then do some personal interrogation."

Callie frowned. "Then the catering angle might be another dead end?"

"Could be, but it's worth pursuing. I would have done so even if Mary hadn't contacted them herself."

"I should have pressed Mary for a name when she said she thought she knew who killed Bernie."

"Don't kick yourself around about that. It's not

likely she found conclusive proof of Bernie's killer in one day when the police have been looking for the Avenger for months and come up with nothing. More likely, she jumped on a hunch and convinced herself she had the man."

Callie stared at him questioningly. "Why would someone kill her unless he was afraid he was about to be exposed?"

"We checked her phone records for the day. She talked to more than twenty people, some of them several times, and I'm fairly sure most of the conversations concerned Bernie. She may have accidentally hit close to the truth and caused the killer to panic."

"And based on that he came to her house, strangled her and threw her into her pool."

"It's the best scenario we have at this point. It's all supposition."

"Which would mean it was likely a guest and not hired help." Callie stood and walked to the railing, staring out into the deep purple twilight. "Mary was vibrant, vivacious and with such a zest for life. Now she's gone, possibly killed by someone she considered a friend."

The pain in Callie's voice crawled inside Max, hacking away at his carefully planned resolve. He walked over and stood beside her, aching to slip an arm around her shoulder, knowing that if he did, he'd release a surge of emotions he might not be able to handle.

"She called and asked me to come over, and I put her off," Callie said. "If I hadn't, she might still be alive."

"It's not you're fault, Callie. None of this is your doing."

"But what if I'd been there?"

She turned to him, her eyes moist with unshed tears.

Max stepped away, fighting the desire that ripped through him with savage force. Callie needed comfort, not the advances of the chief of police who'd come over to question her. Only this had nothing to do with his being a cop. It had to do with the fact he'd had a crazy, impossible thing for Callie Baker ever since the day he'd stood in her wedding party and watched her marry another man.

He dropped his hands to the railing, wrapping his fingers around the smooth wood until his knuckles grew white from the pressure.

"There's a garden party at Judge and Marjorie Craven's house on Saturday afternoon," Callie said, long after the silence had grown awkward. She reached into her pocket and pulled out an embossed invitation. "I think you should go."

Max took a deep breath and tried to figure out how they'd moved from a sensually charged moment to a garden party. "I wasn't invited," he said, thankful for the easy out.

"My invitation is addressed to me and a guest."

Now he was more confused than ever. Callie could find a lot more suitable escorts than him to accompany her to a fancy social affair. "I'll buy you a beer any day of the week, but don't ask me to make small talk with a bunch of women in big-brimmed hats."

"This isn't a date," she said, as if she thought that was going to make him feel better. "At least not in the traditional sense."

"So what is it? Payback for my sins?"

"Garden parties aren't that bad."

"Unless you're talking about getting down and dirty and digging up some damp earth, they are. That's the only kind of gardening activities I'd consider, and I don't have time for those until the Avenger is off the streets."

"That's just it, Max. Mary said if her suspicions were right, the whole town would be shocked at the identity of the killer. I take that to mean the person is not your typical criminal, but someone with money or clout. And the Craven garden party is one of those annual events where everybody who's anybody attends."

"Then they won't miss me."

"But you could miss the Avenger. Chances are good the Avenger was at Mary's party, so it's reasonable to assume he could be at the Cravens' get-together on Saturday afternoon. And even if he's not, he's likely a member of that social circle. You can mingle and chat with people who might know him personally and maybe pick up a lead. If not, what's the worst that can happen?"

The worst? He could lose control and jump Callie's bones in front of everyone who was anybody. "I'll waste an afternoon snacking on cucumber and watercress sandwiches," he said, opting for a more acceptable answer.

"I'll buy you a burger when it's over. It makes sense

for you to go, Max. If the Avenger is there, you should be, too."

He gave it some thought. In theory, it sounded great. In reality, it sucked. He'd stick out like a sore thumb, and he'd feel like a clown at a children's party in the kind of clothes he'd have to wear. And there were other issues as well. "Judge Craven won't like having the chief of police show up and remind everyone that someone was killed at the last big Courage Bay social gathering."

"You won't show up as the chief of police. You'll be my date."

"Same thing. No one's going to believe you and I are an item, not even a one-day item."

She put a hand on his arm. Instinctively he pulled away.

"They'd believe we were dating if you'd…" She hesitated, then changed tactics. "I won't expect anything of you, Max, if that's what frightens you. You don't have to stand around and gaze into my eyes as if we're lovers."

"That's not the problem."

"Then what is the problem?"

The problem was he didn't need to go on a pretend date with Callie. He didn't need his head to come unscrewed when they were in the midst of a murder spree. But there was another problem as well, one that was more pressing.

"I've already told you that I don't want you involved in this investigation in any way."

"I won't be involved," she protested. "I'm just accepting an invitation to a party that I go to every year. One garden party, Max."

He dreaded the thought, yet Callie made a good point. Mixing and mingling in the same social set where the Avenger likely moved with ease might give him some information he couldn't get anywhere else. And the Avenger might well be in attendance.

"Okay, Callie. You've got yourself a date. So what do men wear to the Cravens' garden party?"

"It's dressy, but not formal. White linen suits are popular. Some men wear light colored sports coats. But you can wear whatever you want. They won't throw you out."

"I might embarrass you."

"I'll take my chances."

"Guess I better get out of here before I agree to a night at the opera," Max said.

"I have tickets to one," Callie teased as she walked with him to the front door.

The moment had grown lighter, but he knew the day had been hard on her. "You take care," he said. "And if you need anything tonight, or if you just want to talk, give me a call."

"Thanks."

There was no goodbye kiss, not even on the cheek. He left too fast to risk it. Date or not, he was quite sure Callie wasn't ready to deal with the beast she awakened every time she got close to him. Neither was he.

Already thoughts of Callie were crowding his mind when all his attention should be on catching the Avenger. The passion she aroused in him had been buried inside him for eight long years. All he had to do was keep it in check until this was over.

Right now, as he backed out of her driveway, leaving her alone, that felt like an insurmountable task.

THE SAND SHIFTED beneath his bare feet and the ocean breeze prickled his skin. He loved standing on the beach at night. Liked the feel that it was only he and the crashing waves alone in a world of raw beauty.

Tonight it was more reprieve he sought than solace. He hadn't wanted to kill Mary Hancock, but she'd brought it on herself by getting mixed up with the likes of Bernie Brusco. Women were so gullible where men were concerned. Flash a little money around and flatter them and they bought whatever lies you fed them.

Men like Bernie were masters of fabrication. They destroyed lives to pad their bank accounts, then built walls of pseudorespectability around themselves. Greed. It was all about greed. Money made the world go round and made a mockery of Lady Justice. Common criminals went to jail. The crafty and the rich found a way around it.

It was time to shift the scales in favor of innocent, law abiding citizens. He was sorry about Mary, really sorry, but she was prying into things that were none of her business, and she could have stopped him before he finished his mission.

He felt a quick, stabbing pain at the base of his skull. The sand and the sky seemed to change places, as if he were tumbling from the top of a skyscraper.

Something moved in front of him. White and ghostly. For a second he could have sworn it was Mary Hancock. He closed his eyes tightly. When he opened them again, the figure and the pain were gone.

The attacks came more frequently now. That's why he had to work fast. The mission was all important, and he couldn't let anyone stop him before he'd achieved his goals.

Not Mary Hancock. Not Max Zirinsky.

No one.

CHAPTER SIX

"YOU DO KNOW there's a speed limit in California?" Callie asked, eyeing the speedometer of Mikki's sports car as they drove toward the Keller Center.

Mikki slowed a little, then switched to cruise control. "Not my fault. Happens every time I put on that hot Latin CD."

"Do the cops buy that story when they stop you?"

"No. I usually have to flash a little cleavage," she teased.

Callie knew Mikki was intentionally trying to keep the conversation light. Mikki knew how upset Callie had been since Mary's death and especially since the funeral. But whether Callie talked about the murder or not, it was on her mind. So was her plan. She'd vacillated between coming clean with Mikki or keeping it a total secret, but she really needed a friendly confidante in this.

Callie turned so that she could watch Mikki's expression when she hit her with the latest development. "Max Zirinsky and I are officially dating."

Mikki reached over and switched off the CD player. "Say that again."

"We're officially dating, but before you start planning

the wedding shower, be assured this is all a ruse. Unofficially he's only after one thing, and it's not my body."

"So what's he after?"

"The Avenger." Callie explained the situation. "You're the only one I'm telling this to, Mikki. And I'm only telling you so you won't badger me for details of the romantic encounters we won't be having."

"You might fool yourself with that bunk, but I felt the sparks the other night. If you two spend time together, there will be romance. Not that I'll say I told you so when it happens."

"Oh, no, not you. But I seriously doubt you'll get the chance." Not when Max backed away anytime she even slightly invaded his space.

"When's the first *date?*" Mikki asked.

"This afternoon. We're going to Judge and Marjorie Craven's garden party."

"That explains why you wanted to change our usual afternoon visit to the center to morning. But the good news is I'll get to see you two in action," Mikki said. "I'm going to the garden party as well—also with a date."

"Anyone I know?" Callie asked.

"Not even anyone I know. Abby Hawkins has been after me to meet her son. He's in town for a few weeks. I finally agreed. He's probably a dud and a candidate for an emergency Extreme Makeover."

Callie's stomach muscles tightened. She had no real reason to be suspicious of Jerry Hawkins, especially since it turned out that the accusations he'd made about

Bernie Brusco were true, but the thought of Mikki going out with him definitely made her uneasy.

"He is a dud, isn't he. I can read it in your face. You've met him, and he's a real loser."

"I've met him."

"Should I fake a sudden illness? What's he like?"

"Sandy blond hair. Hard-bodied. Your basic hunk."

"So what's wrong with him?"

"Did I say there was anything wrong with him?"

"Yeah. With your body language. So give, girlfriend."

What *could* she say? Callie wondered. *Oh, I think he could possibly be a serial killer.* That would pretty much cover her suspicions, but without a shred of evidence, Mikki would only laugh off her friend's fears. Besides, Callie couldn't go around accusing people she barely knew of murder.

"He was standing off by himself when I saw him at Mary's party," Callie said. "He looked very bored, so I'm not sure how much fun he'll be." An honest answer and fair to everybody.

"Those fancy social galas can be a real drag." Mikki sounded sympathetic. "Not that I get invited to as many of them as you do. My middle-class background shows up at those things like a flashing neon sign in a cathedral."

"You exaggerate."

"Only a little. Besides, I tend to stand around and look bored occasionally myself—unless, of course, there's a sandy-haired hunk around. I'd like to cut our visit to the center short today if that's okay with you. I have to go home and peruse my closet for something stunning to wear now that you've whet my appetite for my blind date."

So much for that approach. Callie leaned back, tried to concentrate on Jerry Hawkins and ended up with Max Zirinsky's image imposing itself on her thoughts.

She was drawn to him, but it was difficult to know just how much of that attraction was the smouldering remains of that long-ago night when she'd been so needy and disillusioned. She'd changed a lot in eight years. So had Max.

Yet there was still something between them, at least on her part. Maybe not the sizzle Mikki talked about, but at the very least an undercurrent of sensual tension. At the most—well, that remained to be seen. She'd never been good at reading men. Her marriage to Tony was proof of that.

But no matter how Max felt about her as a woman, as of this afternoon, she and Max were a "thing," as Mikki liked to say. She wondered if they'd fool anyone with the charade, especially the Avenger—whoever he was.

Callie hoped he'd be in attendance at the garden party—just not as Mikki's date.

CORTINA AND HER NEWBORN son met Mikki and Callie almost the second they stepped through the wide double doors of the Keller Center. "Isn't he beautiful?" Cortina asked, glowing as she tugged back the blanket so they could see the infant.

"Absolutely beautiful," Mikki agreed.

"Dr. Jackson checked him out again this morning. She said he's perfect. I know his lungs are. And his pooping skills."

"That's all important," Callie said, touching her finger to one of the tiny hands.

"And he must have gained ten ounces since I saw him last week," Mikki said. "What did you decide to name him?"

"Tommy—after my oldest brother."

Callie leaned over to get a closer look. The baby yawned, stretching his little mouth to the limits. "Are we keeping you awake, you precious thing?" she cooed.

"Nothing keeps him awake for long," Cortina said. "Would you like to hold him?"

"I'd love to." Callie opened her arms for the infant, her breath quickening as it always did when she held a baby in her arms. Careful to support the neck and head, she rocked him gently against her breasts.

The infant's hair was dark and curly and his eyes were the shade of a rich café au lait. He stretched and punched his plump little fists into the air. So precious. So warm and cuddly.

"Do you have somewhere to go when you leave here?" Callie asked the new mother.

"I have a job and an apartment." Cortina beamed. "I know it won't be easy as a single parent, but Tommy and I are going to make it just fine."

"Sounds as if you have everything under control," Mikki said.

"I'm getting there, thanks to all of you. Three months ago I was unemployed, there were complications with the pregnancy and I was homeless."

"Glad to know the system works sometimes," Mikki said.

Cortina was definitely one of the Keller Center's success stories. She hadn't eaten in almost two days when she was found sleeping on the steps of a church and brought to the center.

She'd moved to Los Angeles from a rural town in Mississippi with little cash and dreams of making it big in the film industry. Instead she'd met and fallen for the wrong guy. He'd disappeared the minute he'd found out she was pregnant.

Then when she'd developed complications with the pregnancy and couldn't stand on her feet long hours, she'd lost her job as a waitress. It was a story repeated many times at the Keller Center with slight variations.

Tommy started to whimper.

"He's probably hungry," Cortina said, reaching for her son. "It's about the only time he fusses."

Callie's arms felt incredibly empty once she'd returned the squirming neonate to his mother. She'd come to grips with the fact that the tumor and resulting hysterectomy left her unable to have children of her own, but at moments like this...

"Nice to see some of these women get a second chance," Mikki said as Cortina walked away. "Now for the day's challenge, Gail Lodestrum. I'm glad you're the one who has to deal with her."

Gail was most definitely a challenge, Callie thought as her friend headed off in the opposite direction. Gail was scared and depressed and totally overwhelmed with the prospect of giving birth to twins. If anyone in her family had supported her, it would have made things a lot easier for Gail. But no one had. And the teenager refused to name or contact the twins' father, so it was impossible to know if he was willing to help financially or emotionally.

Callie made her way to Gail's room and knocked on the door. There was no answer. "It's me, Dr. Baker. I was hoping we could talk."

Finally the door eased open. Gail's eyes were red and swollen, and the white T-shirt stretched over her bulging belly was smeared with tears and mascara.

"Is something the matter?" Callie asked.

"Everything." Gail backed away, but stopped in front of the wall mirror above her dresser. She placed her hands under her extended belly and stared at her image. "Just look at me. I'm gross."

"You're not gross. Some people say a woman never looks more beautiful than when she's pregnant."

"Yeah, right." Gail collapsed onto the edge of her mattress. "I'm tired of this place."

"There's no reason why you have to stay cooped up inside. Why don't we go out somewhere for a while. We could go to the library or the bookstore and choose something upbeat for you to read."

"There's plenty of books around here already. Besides, I'd have to change clothes, and I don't feel like it."

"Then let's take a walk through the gardens. That would give you a change of scenery."

Gail shrugged her shoulders. "Okay. Whatever."

They went out the back exit and headed toward the narrow stone path that led to a small garden, lush with flowering shrubs and annuals and fed by a stone-dotted brook that originated somewhere in the nearby hillside.

Gail walked slowly along the path, barely lifting her feet. "I don't know why you come here when you don't have to. I know I wouldn't."

"Where would you rather be?" Callie asked.

A butterfly fluttered by and Gail stopped to watch it light on the petals of a hibiscus. "I'd like to be at the beach, hanging out with my friends."

And she should have been, Callie thought. Instead she'd participated in unprotected sex long before she was ready for the kind of responsibility she was facing now. But she hadn't done it alone. "Have you thought any more about telling the babies' biological father about the pregnancy?"

"I've thought about it, but all it would do is ruin his life, too. What's the use of that?"

"The babies are technically as much his as they are yours."

"Yeah, well, technically he's not waddling around with a stomach the size of a watermelon. And he doesn't have to go to the bathroom every ten minutes or wear clothes that would fit a Sumo wrestler."

"Where does he think you are now?"

"Who knows? Who cares? He'll be off to college next month, dating girls who actually have a waist."

"You can get your figure back when the babies are born if you work on it."

"Sure. Whatever."

Gail turned her head away, but not before Callie saw the glint of tears in her eyes. She slipped an arm around Gail's shoulders. "There's nothing wrong with being afraid, Gail. We all are sometimes."

"I'll bet you're not," Gail whimpered, wiping her eyes on her shirttail and exposing her bulging belly.

"Lots of times," Callie assured her.

"What could you be afraid of?"

"Afraid I'll make the wrong decision about a patient's illness or treatment. Afraid I'll fail a friend. And I think of you as a friend."

Gail sniffed and flicked the back of her hand across her eyes. "I'm afraid of what's going to happen to my babies once they're born. I don't know how to take care of them. I don't even know how to take care of me."

"You have choices. I'm sure the counselor has talked to you about that."

"We talked about adoption. But it seems such a copout."

"Not always. It's a difficult situation, but sometimes it's the best one for everybody, especially the babies."

"My babies need a mother who loves them. I used to have one of those. Now she won't even talk to me. I don't blame her. She wanted the perfect daughter. She got me." Gail dropped to a white stone bench nestled beneath a leafy tree. "Do you have children, Dr. Baker?"

"No."

"A husband?"

"No."

"That's too bad. You'd make a good mother. You listen when people talk. That's important."

"Thanks." At one time Callie had imagined herself happily married with children and a medical practice. It had seemed a given back when she'd first fallen in love with Tony. But life was as unpredictable as it was fragile.

Still, she'd been lucky. She had her health and a career she loved. It wasn't everything, but it wasn't bad. She only wished she had answers for Gail, but the teenager would have to find those herself. So Callie just sat in the shade and listened to Gail talk about her fears for herself and her unborn babies.

It wasn't until Mikki and Callie were back in the car and headed toward Courage Bay that Callie's thoughts returned to her pseudodate with Max Zirinsky. She felt a nervous energy at the prospect and wondered whether it was anticipation or caution that caused it. Either way, the afternoon should prove interesting.

THE CRAVENS' GARDEN PARTY might be the highlight of the summer social season, but Max would have preferred a beer, a hot dog and a Dodgers game. How anyone thought that wearing a shirt and tie outside on a day when the temperature was pushing ninety was beyond him.

Not that the women had it so bad. While the men were sweltering in sports coats and dress shirts, the women were prancing about in sundresses with their arms and legs bared. And most of them wore wide-brimmed hats that gave them a little protection from the unrelenting late-afternoon sun.

Callie was the most beautiful woman there. She wore a simple white dress that accentuated her tiny waist and slim hips, and drew stares wherever she went. There had been several pairs of raised eyebrows when she and Max had arrived together. He didn't wonder at the reaction. Callie was gorgeous, wealthy and sophisticated. He was a cop who'd moved up the ranks, but still just your basic cop in every way that mattered.

He caught sight of her now, standing by one of the many fountains scattered about the spacious lawn. She was chatting with Marjorie Craven. Callie saw him watching her and flashed him a dazzling smile that almost made him forget that he was having a miserable time.

"Cocktail, sir?"

"You got a cold beer?" he asked the waiter who'd posed the question.

"I'll check and see if beer is available."

"I'd appreciate it." Max looked around, studying the guests, trying to imagine any one of them as the Avenger. His gaze settled on Leo Garapedian. The guy had been a hell of a chief of detectives before he turned in his badge in favor of a wedding ring. He was here with his wife today. Frankly, Max hadn't expected the marriage or the retirement to last.

But Leo appeared to have made the adjustment from detective to husband of a beautiful, wealthy socialite without a hitch. He was standing near the bar with Judge Craven, laughing at something the judge had said. Leo might not have the look of a cop anymore, but that didn't mean he didn't think like one. No one had gotten more pissed off than Leo when someone he believed guilty got off on a technicality. Leo hadn't been in City Hall when Lorna was shot, but at this point there was no hard evidence that she'd been shot by the Avenger.

Then there was Henry Lalane, standing in a cluster of men, talking animatedly and waving his hands as if he were performing for a jury. He'd spoken to Max today, but the greeting had been extremely cool. And Henry had been present when Lorna Sinke was shot. So had Judge Craven.

The judge left the bar and started walking toward Max, the jacket to his white linen suit swinging jauntily. In his mid-forties, Lawrence Craven was one of the youngest judges in the Courage Bay district. He was a couple of inches shorter than Max, no more than six feet tall, but his dignified manner and self-assured attitude gave him a very imposing presence.

He waited until he was a foot away before speaking. "Quite a surprise seeing you here today, Chief Zirinsky."

"Surprised myself by coming."

"I didn't realize you and Dr. Baker were close friends."

"Callie and I have known each other quite a while," Max said.

"I hope that's why you're here, and it's not because you're expecting trouble."

"Why would I be?"

"These days we're all a little nervous. My wife wanted to cancel the party altogether after Mary was murdered. She and Mary were very close friends. I refused. Canceling anything is letting the Avenger control our lives. As far as I'm concerned, that's the worst thing we could do."

The judge raked his hands through his sleek black hair and straightened his tie, though they both looked impeccable to Max. "Do you have any leads?" he asked, his dark eyes so cold and piercing, the words felt like an accusation to Max.

"Nothing I can talk about," Max said.

"I know the newspapers keep harping on the fact that this Avenger moves about the city with ease and knows everything that's going on, but I don't think he's from around here. Or if he is, he hasn't been living in the area long."

"Why is that?"

"Something Mary said to me the day she was murdered."

The judge's comment came as a surprise to Max. He'd talked to every person Mary had called on her home phone and cell phone that day. Judge Craven had not been on his list.

"What time did she call you?"

"She didn't call. She showed up at my office just before noon. She wanted the name of a good private detective to investigate someone's background. When I asked her who that someone was, she said if her suspicions were right, I'd know soon enough."

"And you think she was investigating the Avenger?"

"Mary believed she was. And since she was murdered a few hours later, I'd say she was probably getting close to the truth. I can't think of a guest at that party whose background we don't know."

"Why didn't you report this before now?"

"I did. I called your department the next morning. Someone took my statement and said they'd make certain it got to the right person. I kept expecting to hear from one of your detectives, but I never did."

Irritation burned in Max's gut. He didn't know who'd taken Craven's statement, but if he found out, someone was going to get their ass chewed out and good. "I didn't get the message," Max admitted. "What else did Mary say?"

"That was pretty much it. I gave her the name of a P.I., but she was killed before she got in touch with him." Craven waved and smiled at a woman near the dance floor, then turned back to Max. "I hope you find the guy soon," he said. "Not only is the man growing more dangerous, but the killings are marring Courage Bay's reputation. They're like a slap in the face to our brave forefathers who founded the town."

They weren't doing much for Judge Craven's political career, either, Max thought with a touch of cynicism. The murders were drawing attention to the fact that Craven was the judge of record when two of the victims had walked. That was the only thing that kept Craven from being high on Max's suspect list. The judge could have bent the law a little and kept them from walking. And bending the law was far less risky than murder for a man as bright and successful as Craven.

They talked for a few more minutes, though not about the Avenger. When the judge walked away, Max went in search of Callie. He found her at the edge of the dance floor, sipping a drink the color of a sunset and swaying her hips to the music.

"I've been looking for you," she said. "May I have this dance?"

Fortunately it was a slow one. Max was pretty sure he looked like a spastic frog when he tried those fast numbers where you never touched your partner. He took her hands and tried to maneuver the floor to the beat of the music while holding her a safe distance away.

Only there was no safe distance, not with Callie's hands linked with his and her perfume flooding his senses. Her nearness was more intoxicating than straight whiskey, and when she moved closer the hunger that built inside him was downright frightening.

A make-believe date. But there was nothing make believe about Callie. She was all woman, soft, yielding, and with every sway of her body against his, his need for her jumped another notch higher.

He willed his mind to concentrate on the weird shape of the singer's mustache, or the ridiculous feathered hat of a woman dancing nearby, or the way the open tent was fastened to the stakes. Anything except the feel and fragrance of Callie.

When the song was over, he sucked in a ragged breath and escorted her off the floor.

"I hate that," Callie said, tugging him to a stop.

"I'm sorry. I guess I should have warned you that I'm not much of a dancer."

"I'm talking about the way Jerry's making a play for Mikki." She nodded toward the dance floor as the small band started a new song.

Max scanned the dancers until he spotted the couple. "Mikki looks like she's happy," he said, noting that her head was on her partner's shoulder, and there was a dreamy look on her face.

"He's a blind date. She knows absolutely nothing about him."

"I thought you said his mother was a regular volunteer at the hospital and a friend of yours."

"His mother's my friend. Not him. He could be the Avenger for all we know."

"So could anyone here."

"Did you investigate him?" she asked.

"I ran a check. He's had a couple of speeding tickets and numerous parking violations, but no felony charges."

"What does he do?"

"He owns a very successful construction business in Sacramento. I think you're getting worked up over nothing."

"Maybe, but I have this feeling about him. I can't explain it, but I don't trust him."

"Did you tell Mikki that?"

"Not yet."

"Then why don't you wait and let me do some more checking on him. If I find anything that looks suspicious, I'll let you know."

"I guess I can live with that." But she didn't sound happy as she turned back to the couple in time to see Jerry whisper something in Mikki's ear that made her smile and snuggle closer.

"Here comes Janice Lalane," Callie warned in a low voice. "Stick close, smile and act as if you like me, boyfriend."

"I'll give it my best shot," Max promised.

CALLIE WAS TOTALLY BUMMED out by the time she slipped out of the white sundress and curled up in front of the TV for an old episode of *Friends*. If Max had learned anything of value at the Cravens' party, he'd kept it to himself. He'd hardly talked at all on the drive back to her place, and had refused her invitation to come in for a drink.

He clearly didn't want to become involved with her in any personal way. She should be grateful for that instead of letting it get to her. Pickering trotted over and licked her hand. She scratched him behind his ear and he wagged his tail fast and furiously.

"It's a woman thing, Pickering. We just can't stand the thought that we can be resisted."

Mikki wasn't likely having any thoughts of rejection tonight, not the way Jerry Hawkins had held her while they danced. Callie had half a mind to call her friend and warn her that the guy might not be what he seemed. But Max was right. She was probably overreacting.

If only Jerry hadn't sounded so venomous when he'd spoken about Bernie that night. It was clear Jerry didn't think the man deserved to live. His remarks might have made a little more sense if the two men had lived in the same town, but Bernie operated out of L.A., and Jerry lived in Sacramento.

And why had Abby mentioned her daughter Elizabeth several times and not once mentioned Jerry until Callie had told her she'd met him? There were just too many things that didn't add up with him, like the fact that he was boating and dancing and going to parties when he was supposed to be recovering from some kind of injury.

Restless, Callie turned out the lights and walked out to the pool. Her deck area was separated from her neighbors' property by a privacy fence, making it perfect for skinny-dipping. She slipped out of her yellow silk robe and let it fall to the tiles before climbing onto the diving board and taking a plunge into the cool water.

Pickering got down on his haunches and chewed on one of his rubber toys while she swam lap after lap until the stress of the day dissolved into a gentle ache in her arms and shoulders.

Rolling over, she floated on her back, staring up at the stars and the crescent moon. Finally she started to climb out, then caught a reflection in the pool that sent frightening images rushing through her mind.

Mary's naked body at the bottom of the pool.

A scream stalled at the back of Callie's throat and an icy chill settled deep in her bones.

Pickering rose, as if sensing her fear, but instead of coming to her, he walked to the edge of the deck, lifted his head and stared in the direction of the beach.

He growled threateningly and Callie grabbed for her robe and pulled it around her, suddenly struck with the sensation that someone was nearby, in the darkness, watching her house, waiting for her to appear.

Was this what it had been like for Mary before she was murdered?

CHAPTER SEVEN

CALLIE RACED INTO the house and with trembling fingers locked all the doors. Her nerves were shot from finding Mary's body, and she knew her imagination was likely working overtime. But even inside with the doors locked, she couldn't shake the feeling that someone had been watching her.

This kind of paranoia was not like her, but still, as she slid her arms through a heavy robe from the downstairs closet, she felt chilled and uneasy. She considered calling Max and having him send a patrolman by to check the area around the house, but she was afraid he'd come himself. She didn't want him to see her like this. If she threw herself into his arms, he'd hold her and make her feel safe—then run away for another eight years.

Besides, she paid well for the neighborhood security system. There was no reason not to use it. She punched in the number and asked to have one of the security guards check around her house for signs of a voyeur or trespasser.

She'd moved into this house right before her divorce from Tony. This was the first time she'd felt threatened.

The area was private, and the beach was frequented only by the residents who lived along this section of the road and boaters who occasionally moored in the bay.

Still, she was uneasy as she waited, and started when Pickering barked and ran to the door before the bell chimed. She peeked through the peephole. The guy was in uniform and wearing a gun at his waist. Still, to be on the safe side, Callie turned on the intercom. "Could you show me some ID?"

"Sure thing, Dr. Baker." He pulled out his wallet and held it so she could read his name and see the Lansing Security logo. "Are you okay?"

"Yes, but I had the distinct feeling someone was nearby when I was in the pool, and my dog was growling at the fence as if someone was out there. To be honest, I can't imagine anyone could see over the fence, but I'd appreciate it if you'd have a look around."

"I'll check everything out and get back to you."

"Thanks."

She walked the floor as she waited, trying to be sensible and objective about this. She knew there was some risk involved when she'd offered to help Max. But Mary had been her friend. Callie couldn't just ignore that fact.

And even if the Avenger had been at the Craven party and hadn't bought the idea that Max was her date, there was no reason to think he'd bother with her. What threat did she pose for him?

The doorbell startled her again, although she'd been expecting it.

"I did a thorough check and couldn't find any sign of an intruder. If there was someone out there, he's long gone now."

"It was probably nothing," she said, trying to sound a lot more assured than she felt.

"Always best to be safe, and that's what we're here for. Do you want me to check the inside of the house before I go?"

"No. If someone were in here, Pickering would let me know. He'd probably lick the intruder to death, but at least I'd know he was around."

"A dog's the best warning system there is. And he might surprise you. A dog can sense danger. He wouldn't let anyone hurt you without first taking a few chunks out of the guy."

Pickering barked his agreement. The security guard reassured her again, then walked back to his car.

Callie filled a glass with cold water, sipped it slowly, then walked upstairs behind Pickering, who was bounding ahead. She'd spent entirely too much time this week thinking of murders and avengers—and Max. And she was too physically and emotionally drained to deal with any of it now.

In spite of the fear she'd felt earlier, she drifted into a semisleep a few minutes after her head hit the pillow. She was back at the garden party. The women were dressed in shimmering gowns the color of blood. The men all carried guns.

Callie jerked awake and sat up straight in bed. Moonlight filtered through the curtains, casting a stream of silver across her breasts. Moonlight and murder.

The contrast was as bizarre as her life had become. And she had a feeling that things were about to get a lot worse.

MAX SAT IN HIS OFFICE on Sunday morning nursing a cup of strong black coffee and staring at the crime-scene photos and autopsy reports he'd spread across his desk.

Dylan Deeb. Bruce Nepom. Lorna Sinke. Carlos Esposito.

Their deaths spanned almost a seven-month period, one every two to three months. Although all four were suspected criminals, there was no proof they'd been killed by the man known as the Avenger.

Bernie Brusco and Mary Hancock had been murdered within days of each other. Bernie had been involved in illegal activities, but the only motive Max could see for killing Mary was that the Avenger was afraid she knew something that could lead to his identification. But what was it he thought she knew?

When Max had become chief of police, he could never have imagined such a killing spree in quiet Courage Bay. And the Avenger wasn't the only one out for justice. The previous month, Nora Keyes, the police bomb squad specialist, and Sam Prophet, the fire department's arson investigator, had barely missed being victims themselves of an arsonist known as the Trigger. Firefighters at the downtown station were still reeling from the discovery that the arsonist was Bud Patchett, their popular mechanic.

Bud's brother Tim was injured while test-driving a car containing a defective computer chip and died shortly after. When the company Tim worked for refused to accept responsibility for his death, Bud set out on a personal quest for revenge.

Bud had been killed when the cell phone he'd rigged with explosives had detonated in his own truck. One murderer gone. One still to find.

Max picked up a pen and started randomly jotting down a projected profile of the Avenger. He'd likely be male, since he'd been strong enough to strangle one victim and bludgeon another to death. He knew how to use a gun, but wasn't a hundred percent accurate, especially if he was responsible for shooting Lorna Sinke.

His firearms expertise might indicate military experience or policework. He'd likely be involved in the criminal justice system, and might have experienced some perceived injustice himself.

The most confusing aspect of the murders was that there was no pattern to the types of crimes. They ranged from sexual exploitation to drug dealing.

Max tore off the sheet, wadded it into a ball and tossed it into the wastebasket. He printed the word *suspects* at the top of the next sheet.

Number one: every cop on his force. The nature of their job made them all suspects. But Max had no real reason to believe any one of them was guilty.

Number two: Leo Garapedian, former chief of detectives. The guy thought the judicial system coddled criminals and was livid whenever a criminal walked on a technicality. But Leo worked off his stress at the gym. Besides, he was in love. No reason for him to go off the deep end.

There was Judge Lawrence Craven. In his prime. Successful. Followed the law to the letter. Hard to believe he'd just up and start killing suspected criminals. The guy was too ambitious to risk his career.

And then there was the district attorney. Henry Lalane had been hard on crime before his daughter was killed. Now he was rabid on the issue. And he had been in the room when Lorna Sinke was shot. But Max needed something more solid than circumstance and supposition.

He needed a weapon, DNA, an eyewitness, something concrete to hang a case on. Or a scrap of information to put him on the right track. He'd hoped to get that at the garden party he'd attended with Callie, but the only information he'd received had been Mary's remarks to Judge Craven about being on the trail of the Avenger. Max seriously doubted there was any basis to her suspicions.

Callie was worried about Jerry Hawkins, but a successful building contractor who lived in Sacramento seemed an unlikely candidate for Courage Bay's serial killer.

Max pushed his notes aside and shoved away from his desk. Just the thought of Callie and things started revving up inside him. She turned him on the way no other woman ever had. And not just physically, though getting a hard on every time she got close was a given. She burrowed deep under his skin and just stayed there, ready to distract him at the most inconvenient times.

Like right now, when he had a murderer to stop.

It would be easy to give in when he was with her, especially when she seemed so receptive to him. But for her it would just be a date, a nice dinner and a bottle of wine. A couple of kisses. Maybe they'd make love.

Damn. Thinking about it twisted him inside out. Eight years later and he still wasn't over a kiss. If he made love to her, he was pretty sure he'd never recover.

That's why he had to keep his distance. He was too damn old to fall apart over Callie Baker again.

CALLIE WAS GRATEFUL when Mikki called midmorning on Sunday and asked her to meet at the country club for a couple of sets of tennis. There was nothing like exercise to clear the mind and get the kinks out of the body. And dispel the threat she felt hovering on the edges of her awareness.

The brunch crowd had eaten and gone by the time they finished their sets and took quick showers in the change room.

"Let's eat on the veranda," Mikki said. "It's too gorgeous to stay indoors."

"Fine by me."

They found a table in the shade with a view of the first tee box. "What can I get you to drink?" the waitress asked as she handed them the menu.

"Ice water," they answered in unison.

"You must have been on the courts," the woman said. "Tennis players always want water. Golfers are usually ready for a serious drink."

"Two sets," Mikki confirmed. She glanced at the menu. "Any interesting specials?"

"The soup's a corn and smoked chicken chowder. People have been raving about that. There's a summer tomato and shrimp salad with balsamic-cabernet vinaigrette, roasted garlic, blue cheese and fresh herbs. And there's a tuna steak with Chef Pierre's secret sauce."

"Tough choices," Mikki said. "I was thinking about a club sandwich, but everything you mentioned sounds yummy."

"It is. Let me get your water while you think about it."

"The soup and salad sounds tempting," Callie said, scanning the rest of the menu. "But then I love the egg dishes on the brunch menu."

Callie settled on eggs Benedict. Mikki ordered the soup, salad and a dozen fried oysters with fries.

"How did the date go with your sexy police chief?" Mikki asked once the waitress had walked away.

"I'm not sure if we fooled anyone, especially since we were barely together. Max spent most of the afternoon mingling with other people."

"Wasn't that the plan?"

Callie nodded. "I just thought we might mingle together a bit more."

"I saw the two of you dancing."

"One dance, and even then he would have kept daylight between us if I hadn't forced him to come a bit closer."

"Knowing all eyes were on you in that scrumptious white dress probably made him nervous. So let's get down to the good stuff. What happened when you got back to your place?"

"Absolutely nothing. I think he set a new record for the sprint to his car." Callie took a sip of water, deciding not to mention that she'd called security to do a grounds check last night. No reason to worry Mikki when the guard hadn't found anything amiss.

"How did it go with you and Jerry?" she asked, ready to change the subject.

"Great. He's really a neat guy. Smart, funny and charming."

This was not what Callie wanted to hear, especially not in the bubbly tone Mikki usually reserved for hot firemen.

"You didn't…never mind. It's none of my business."

"Sure it is. We're best friends. But the answer is no. We didn't do the deed, though we probably would have if it had been left to me. One kiss and I was putty in his big, gorgeous hands. Definitely the hottest blind date I've ever had."

"I think you should go slow with this, Mikki. You hardly know the man."

"When have you ever known me to go slow with anything?"

Never, and that worried Callie all the more. "Did he say what kind of injury he was recovering from?"

"He never mentioned an injury."

"Abby said that's why he's in town."

"I just figured he was on vacation. He's part owner of a construction company in Sacramento. Hawkins and Reilly Design and Construction. They build skyscrapers. How cool is that?"

"Cool, but that's another reason you don't want to get in too deep with him. He'll be going back to Sacramento soon."

"Why do I get the feeling you know something you're not telling me. He's not married, is he? Or gay?"

Callie traced a line of condensation on her glass. "You know I'd tell you if I found out something like that. It's just…"

"Say it, Callie. What is it about Jerry that you don't like?"

"I didn't say I don't like him. It's just that with a serial killer throwing the city into terror, I think you should be careful about dating people you don't know anything about."

"When did you become so paranoid? Give me a break. It's not like Jerry's some guy I picked up in a bar. He's Abby's son. He's no more the Avenger than I am."

Her concern did sound paranoid when put that way, Callie silently admitted.

The waitress returned with Mikki's soup. Mikki took a few bites, then toyed with the spoon, making circles in the thick chowder.

"What's wrong with the soup?" Callie asked.

"Nothing. I'm just not very hungry."

"Could you say that again? I know I heard it wrong."

"Soup's fine. I just don't have my usual appetite for some reason." Then, apparently forgetting Callie's reservations about her blind date, Mikki started talking about Jerry again.

The waitress arrived with the rest of their order. In spite of Callie's uneasiness over Jerry Hawkins, she dove into her salad. The morning's exercise had left her famished. Mikki forked a bite of salad into her mouth, then stared into space.

Silent and experiencing a loss of appetite? Mikki had it bad, Callie realized. Max had said there was no reason to consider Jerry a suspect, and Mikki obviously agreed. But paranoid or not, Callie couldn't shake her doubts. There were too many things about Jerry Hawkins that didn't add up.

She might be able to check out one of them herself. Her med school friend Lindsey Evans was chief of staff at one of the major hospitals in Sacramento. She could find out if Jerry Hawkins had been treated in her hospital for an injury. If so, Callie would be satisfied he had a valid reason for being in town and would feel a lot better about his dating Mikki.

She took one last bite of salad, then pushed her plate away. Her appetite had vanished, too. Besides, she was eager to make the phone call to Lindsey. Sunday afternoon should be a good time to catch her at home, where she'd have time to talk.

"... my luck."

Callie looked up. She'd been so lost in her own thoughts, she'd missed the first part of Mikki's statement. "I'm sorry. I missed that."

"I was just lamenting my luck," Mikki said. "Finally I meet a man I can go for who's not gay, married or carting a ton of baggage, and he has to live in Sacramento." She sighed. "Still, it could be worse."

It could be a lot worse, Callie thought. He could be the Avenger.

CALLIE DROVE to the hospital to retrieve Lindsey's number from her office Rolodex. Fortunately, Lindsey was home, relaxing with her husband, Drake, and their toddler daughter.

"Jerry Hawkins." Lindsey repeated the name Callie had given her. "Would that be Gerald Parker Hawkins of Hawkins and Reilly Design and Construction?"

"As a matter of fact, it would. You sound as if you know him."

"Drake's done some business with him and I got to know him last year. So, how do you know Jerry?"

"He's in Courage Bay for a few weeks visiting his mother and recovering from an injury."

"What kind of injury?"

"That's what I was hoping you could check out for me."

"I don't understand. Is he a patient of yours?"

"No." This was turning out to be more complicated than she'd expected. "He's dating a friend of mine, and I just have a feeling he's lying about the injury, mainly because his activity level doesn't seem affected in any way."

"So you think he might be lying to her about other things, like having a wife in Sacramento."

"Something like that." Not being completely honest with Lindsey bothered Callie immensely, but she couldn't let Mikki continue to date Jerry if he posed a threat to her.

"I don't know anything about Jerry being injured, but his partner fell from some scaffolding last fall. The accident left him brain dead and comatose. He hung on for weeks before he died, and Jerry was at his bedside almost constantly. That's when I got to know him. He's quite a guy, and he's not married."

And here Callie had been imagining him capable of cold-blooded murder.

"He felt really guilty about the accident," Lindsey said. "He took it hard when his partner died. Maybe that's what he's getting over."

"Why would he feel guilty?"

"He was on the scaffolding with his partner when he fell, and Jerry blames himself for not saving him. He came so close to reaching him that from the ground, it looked as if Jerry had pushed him, at least that's what a passerby reported. His partner fell four floors onto the concrete. It was amazing he lived at all."

From the ground, it looked as if he'd pushed him.

Those were the only words that registered in Callie's mind, and they echoed like an avalanche thundering through a mountain pass. If Jerry was their Avenger, his killing spree might have started with his partner, then spread to Courage Bay.

Realistically she knew Jerry could be as innocent as she was. Yet that didn't stop her mind from coming up with all kinds of macabre possibilities.

She had to talk to Max. After a hurried goodbye to Lindsey, Callie punched in Max's number. The second he answered, she gave him a blow-by-blow of what she'd just learned.

"Slow down, Callie. You're not making any sense."

"Then meet me at the Courage Bay Bar and Grill. I can explain better in person."

"When?"

"An hour from now." That would give her time to see a few patients while she was here at the hospital.

"I'll be there."

Callie leaned forward and rested her elbows on her desk. She had to get a grip, stop obsessing over these murders and get back to her own life. Medicine instead of murder. Patients instead of suspects. Calm control instead of suspicions and fear.

But there was one suspicion she couldn't overcome. Paranoid or not, she had to convince Mikki not to see Jerry Hawkins again until they knew for certain that he was not the Avenger.

MARJORIE CRAVEN strolled through her garden on Sunday afternoon, silently lamenting that her annual party had not seemed nearly as pleasurable as in recent years. She just couldn't get Mary's death out of her mind and she was certain many of the other guests couldn't, either.

Max Zirinsky's presence hadn't done anything to boost people's spirits, either. Several guests were convinced that Max was there because he suspected one of them of being the Avenger. Marjorie had to agree, especially since Max wasn't the type of man she'd expect a refined, sophisticated woman like Callie to date. But he was very masculine—too rugged for Marjorie's tastes, but sexy all the same. And she'd thought him a very effective chief of police until the city had been plagued with so many unsolved murders.

Marjorie stooped and picked up a paper napkin trapped in the foliage of one of her prize rosebushes. She dropped it into the small bag she was carrying for just that purpose.

The cleanup crew had done an excellent job, but there were always a few things they missed. Scraps of paper stuck in the bushes, the odd crumpled napkin and used tissue blown into the flower beds.

Last year she'd found Henry Lalane's American Express card in a potted fern. She'd never understood that one. And then two years ago she'd discovered a phone number scribbled on a napkin. A tryst in the making, she'd gleefully imagined, and she'd looked up all her friends' numbers to see if there was a match.

Lawrence had made fun of her and teased her of being jealous that one of her friends might be engaged in a little extracurricular activity. But that would never happen, Marjorie thought. Lawrence was all the man she needed.

A bluebird sang to her as she neared the cliff that bordered the back of the garden. She stopped close to the edge and looked out over the bay. The view was magnificent. It was the main reason she and Lawrence had bought this house the day it came on the market, even though there was no beach access.

Marjorie stopped to watch a squirrel scurrying up a skinny birch that grew precariously among the rocks, then forgot the animal as she ran to grab a small square of paper before it sailed over the cliff. She did so hate litter.

Curious as always, Marjorie looked to see what was written on the note. It was a list of typed names. She noticed Bernie Brusco's and Mary Hancock's at once, then realized she was looking at a list of all the people allegedly killed by the Avenger. Someone was obviously keeping score, though they'd added more names than even the media were attributing to the guy.

Only one name wasn't typed. It was scribbled in red just below Mary's name. Number eight.

Marjorie's hands tightened on the piece of paper, the same way her chest was tightening. This was a list of victims. But the last name on the list was still alive. Clutching the slip of paper, she rushed back to the house, wishing Lawrence was home and not playing golf with his buddies.

Not that his being home would have changed anything. This was a matter for the police.

MAX WAS CLEARING off his desk, preparing to go meet Callie, when one of the younger police officers stuck his head in the door of his office.

"I know you're not officially *in,* but I have Judge Craven's wife on the phone. She asked for you, says she has some important information on the Avenger murder case. You want me to take her statement or do you want to take her call?"

"I'll take it."

"Line three."

He picked up the phone. "Max Zirinsky."

"I'm so glad you're in. I found this note and... It's a list, Max."

There was no missing the frenzied panic in her voice. "What kind of list?"

"Names."

She read them off, her voice becoming shriller with each one. Except for the first on the list, the names were those of the Avenger's victims.

"Where did you find this list?"

"At the far end of the garden. I caught it just before it blew over the edge of the cliff."

So it could have fallen from the pocket of any of her two hundred plus guests yesterday, Max realized. And it didn't mean a thing. The Avenger was the talk of the town these days. Too many people thought he was some kind of hero. And lots more were speculating about the who, how and when of the next victim.

"I appreciate the call," he said, "but I don't think you

have a thing to worry about. Anyone could have made that list. It doesn't mean the Avenger was at your garden party."

"There's one more name, Chief Zirinsky. At the end of the list. It's not typed like the rest of them. In fact, it's printed in large almost childish letters. I think...I think it could be the name of the next victim."

That piqued Max's interest. "Whose name is it?"

"Dr. Callie Baker."

CHAPTER EIGHT

MAX WAS FIFTEEN MINUTES late arriving at the Courage Bay Bar and Grill. He'd stopped off at the Cravens' on the way over and picked up the note.

It was safely stored in plastic now, but he was doubtful he'd be able to retrieve any prints off it other than Marjorie Craven's. If she hadn't messed up his chances when she'd handled it, the friction of blowing across the grass and plants for almost twenty-four hours probably had.

He spotted Callie the minute he stepped through the door. She was sitting at a table with two nurses. A million emotions seemed to hit him at once. He tamped them down as best he could. He had to play this cool.

Lots of luck. When had he ever played anything cool where Callie was concerned?

She introduced him to the two nurses, then followed him to the farthest table from the noisy bar area. There weren't a lot of heavy drinkers this time of day, but cops, firefighters and hospital workers stopped in for a beer or a cup of coffee when their shifts were over, and most hung around awhile to shoot the breeze.

"Sorry I'm late," Max said, sliding into the chair at a right angle to Callie's.

"No problem. It gave me time to catch up on a little hospital gossip. Nothing too spicy. I think the nurses keep that among themselves. We doctors only get the routine stuff, like who's getting married and who's trying to get pregnant."

"You sounded upset when you called," he said. "I'm guessing it didn't have anything to do with hospital gossip."

"No. It's about Jerry—" She stopped talking when a young waiter Max hadn't seen before stopped at their table.

"What can I get you two?"

Callie ordered a cappuccino. Max went for plain coffee. Neither ordered food, though Max hadn't eaten since breakfast—a couple of slices of cold pizza he'd found on the bottom shelf of his refrigerator.

No use to order food now. Ever since Mrs. Craven had told him Callie's name was on the note, his stomach had felt as if it was being stomped by someone wearing army boots.

"Were you referring to Jerry Hawkins?" Max asked, when the waiter stepped away from the table.

Callie nodded. "I had lunch with Mikki today. He was all she could talk about."

"I take it they hit it off yesterday."

"Apparently."

"You don't sound too happy about that," he said, reading the concern in her voice and facial expression.

"I know you said Jerry checked out, Max, but I have this feeling about him that I can't shake, and it doesn't seem unfounded to me. The first time he attended a Courage Bay social gathering with his mother, there was a murder attempt on a man that he admitted he'd like to see dead. And I'm not the only one he said that to. He told Mikki that the guy who killed Bernie should get a medal."

"Lots of people in Courage Bay probably think that way now that they know how Bernie made his millions."

"Maybe," Callie agreed, "but I've learned more about Jerry, and it's possibly even more condemning."

Max listened to the story of Jerry's partner falling from the scaffolding. The timing hit him as much as anything. Jerry's partner had died last fall, and the first of the murders attributed to the Avenger had occurred in November.

At least that was what he'd believed until Marjorie Craven had given him the list of victims. The first name on the list was Dr. George Yube. Max would have to go back and give that case another look.

If Jerry had killed his partner in rage over some real or perceived injustice, it might have triggered the string of Avenger-type killings.

The waiter returned with two steaming mugs of coffee.

"Did you mention any of this to Mikki?" Max asked while Callie stirred a package of sweetener into her brew.

"Not yet. I wanted to talk to you about it first."

"Good. I'll follow up, but you have to leave this to me, Callie. You've done enough." Too much, if the victim list in his pocket had been written by the Avenger.

"I can't ignore the situation, Max. If Jerry is a deranged killer, then dating him could put Mikki in danger."

"I'll handle it. If on the very outside chance he does turn out to be the Avenger, Mikki is in a lot less danger if she doesn't suspect a thing. Trust me on this, Callie."

She exhaled slowly, her body language indicating her consent would be a major concession. "I'll try—for a day or two. That's all I can promise."

He took a sip of his coffee and tried to get his thoughts together. She was worried about Mikki, but it was Callie Max was worried about.

"I stopped by Judge Craven's house on the way over here," Max said.

She peered at him over the rim of her cup. "Police business?"

"Yeah. Marjorie Craven called to tell me she'd found a note blowing about her garden this afternoon."

Callie leaned in closer, obviously picking up on the change in his tone. "What kind of note?"

"A list of the Avenger's victims."

"Who needs a list? The names are mentioned on every local newscast and in at least one newspaper article a day."

Max reached in his shirt pocket and pulled out the clear plastic bag, careful to touch only the edges. "This list is a little different. It's got a couple of extra names on it."

"Whose names?"

"Dr. George Yube for one."

"Why would the list include him? Wasn't he killed by Felix Moody?"

"The evidence was fairly conclusive that Moody was the trigger man, but we never heard Moody's side of the story since he was killed before we had a chance to take him to trial. And sometimes even what appears to be solid evidence can be misleading."

"Why do I have the feeling there's something you're not telling me?"

Her gaze locked with his, and the vulnerability in her soft brown eyes made his heart plunge to his worn loafers. "There's a possibility the note was written by the Avenger."

"Why would you think that?" she asked. "Anyone could have written down the names of the victims and unknowingly included Dr. Yube. After all, he fits the profile of the Avenger's victims. He walked away from a murder trial on a technicality."

"I have to consider all possibilities."

"You don't seem inclined to consider Jerry Hawkins a suspect."

"I never said that. I just don't want you doing the investigating."

"So who else's name is on the list Marjorie found?" she asked again.

He held the bag so that she could see the list through the clear plastic, then watched as shock drew deep furrows in her brow and left her beautiful mouth hanging open.

But only for a second. As she took a deep breath, the look of shock was replaced with one of fury. "What kind of sick joke is this? I'm not a criminal. I don't even cheat on my taxes."

"It may not be a joke. You took me to the Cravens' garden party. If the Avenger was there, he may have seen my presence as a threat. That's why I have to consider it possible this list was written by the Avenger and he added your name to it."

"If he did, he might not have done it just because I took you to the party," she said. "He could think Mary told me something before he killed her."

"That's possible." Callie was shrewd, which was why Max had to level with her. She'd never settle for less than the truth. "Anyone could have written that note and scribbled your name on it, but since there's a chance it was the Avenger, we have to react to it that way."

"Which means act as if he has me targeted as his next victim." She toyed with her spoon, letting a drop of coffee drip from it onto her paper napkin. "I thought I had an intruder last night, Max. Not inside my house, but outside. It could have been the Avenger, casing the joint so to speak, deciding if I'd be an easy target."

Damn. He clenched and unclenched his fists while she gave him the details. Max struggled to keep from losing control completely and pounding his fists into the table. He'd left her alone last night, a mistake he wouldn't make again.

"It doesn't add up," she said. "Why would the Avenger type the names on the list? He knows who he killed without a visual reminder. It's not as if he's as prolific as the Green River Killer."

"It's not uncommon for serial killers to take a trophy from their victims. We haven't noticed that in this case, so perhaps the Avenger keeps a typed list to remind him of his successes."

"Kind of like a gunfighter's notches," she mused. "But my name's not typed."

"And I plan to make sure you don't become a notch."

She narrowed her eyes and stared at the list. "I think he's running scared, Max. See how garish and misshapen the letters in my name are. It's as if he could barely control his hand. I'll bet he knows his luck has to run out soon."

"Running scared will only make him less cautious and more dangerous, Callie. That's why you can't take any chances until the Avenger is in custody or we find out that he didn't write this note."

Callie stiffened her back and sat up straighter. "I'm not going to give up my life and just hide out from the lunatic."

"No, but you can't run around unprotected, either. The guy's not only cunning, he's a good shot. He used a high-powered rifle to take Bernie out."

"I guess I could hire a bodyguard."

"That won't be necessary. I'll assign someone to stick by you from the time you leave for work in the morning until you get back home at night." Max would feel a whole lot better with one of his top cops watching over her than he would with some L.A. bouncer turned security guard, which was about all you could find these days. But he would have to be very careful who he chose to guard her.

"That takes care of my days," she said. "What about my nights?"

He gulped down the rest of his coffee and returned the note to his pocket, preparing himself for an argument that he had no intention of losing—and an emotional entanglement that he had no chance to win.

"You won't have to worry about the nights. I'm moving in with you, starting now."

"YOU CAN'T DO THAT!" The protest flew from Callie's mouth before Max's words fully sank in. She'd lived alone for years. She swam naked, slept naked, roamed around the house naked.

Not that wearing clothes would be that much trouble, but if he moved in with her, Max would be there when she stumbled down the stairs for coffee with morning breath. He'd be there when she cut her toenails and gave Pickering a bath. He'd be there…all the time.

"It's out of the question, Max. I'm used to my privacy. You're used to yours."

"You can just go about your business and pretend I'm not there. I'll take the guest room. If you don't have one, I can sleep on the couch."

Sure. Just pretend he wasn't there, when her sensual awareness level soared every time he came into view.

"One other thing, Callie. I don't want anyone to know that you may have been targeted."

"And you don't think they'll notice I have a cop at my heels all day and the chief of police sleeping at my house?"

"You won't have a cop. You'll have an assistant, a medical student, an intern, a nurse. He won't be in uniform, so introduce him any way that works for you."

That might be doable. She did have medical students assist her from time to time. "That would explain having someone in my office, not sleeping in my house."

"You've set the stage for that already. You took me to a garden party."

"It's a big move from dating to living together. Besides, I'm not the type to just move in with someone."

"Then tell them we're engaged."

"It doesn't matter what I say. No one will buy that we're living together."

"It's not a matter of their believing we're living together. We *will* be living together."

His voice was huskier than a minute ago, raw the way her nerves felt. She was reacting to the wrong things. It was the threat from a killer that should be claiming her thoughts, not whether or not she could handle living with a man for whom she'd carried a secret torch all these years. It would be different if he felt the same, but there was no indication that he did.

But her name was on a victim list. She had no choice but to deal with the haunting memories and the unexplainable desire he stirred. "Okay, Max. We'll try this your way."

"You won't have to worry. I'll keep you safe, Callie." He reached across the table and laid his hands on top of hers. "I promise you that I'll keep you safe."

She didn't doubt for a second that he'd keep his promise. He'd keep her safe from the Avenger. Protecting her heart would be up to her.

HE CHECKED THE RIGHT POCKET in his suit jacket for the third time, then went back and checked all the pockets in the jacket and the trousers he'd worn yesterday. The list was missing.

If someone found it, they'd know he'd targeted Callie Baker as his next victim. That might make her murder difficult, and things were already getting far more complicated than he'd intended.

His perfect plan was going awry. He'd never meant to kill anyone who didn't deserve the death sentence, but first Mary and now Callie had gone snooping into things that didn't concern them, planting land mines in his playing field. But he couldn't let them destroy his mission.

Three more kills. That's all he had planned. Not murders, as the media proclaimed, but justice, meted out swiftly and equitably the way it was supposed to be.

The mission was all important. It was his legacy. And he would not stop until it was completed and justice was served.

CALLIE WAS STILL REELING from the latest developments as she stood in the guest bedroom while Max unpacked the few changes of clothes he'd brought with him. She'd thought the act of watching him calmly put his things away in her closet and bureau would make this move seem less provocative and remind her of the danger she faced. So far it wasn't working.

The only man she'd lived with other than her father had been Tony, and they hadn't moved in together until after the wedding. She'd thankfully forgotten a lot of the day-to-day details about her life with Tony, but she knew the sexual attraction had never been this strong.

But then she and Tony had had sex to defuse the tension. So far Max had managed to avoid so much as an incidental brush of shoulders or hands with her. Not that he was cold or brusque. He just didn't show any sign that sleeping in the same house as Callie was anything more than part of his job.

She'd pretty much ruled out the intimidation factor as the reason he avoided any hint of intimacy. Max wasn't the type to be either impressed or deterred by her inherited wealth or the fact that she was a successful physician. And it surely wasn't because she'd once been married to his cousin, not with Tony on his third wife.

So either the sexual tension that insinuated itself into her very pores when he was around was one-sided, or else Max had his own reasons for playing this so damn cool. Her instincts told her it was the latter, but that could be wishful thinking on her part, a way to make her feel less like a schoolgirl with a crush.

"I'm going to change into something more comfortable, then I'll be downstairs if you need anything," she said, deciding that standing here watching him unpack his underwear wasn't helping matters.

He nodded. "You don't have to entertain me."

"I'm not sure I could," she admitted truthfully. "I would like to talk about the case against the Avenger, though. If I'm going to be in the middle of it, I think I deserve to know what you've learned so far in your investigation."

"That will take about five minutes."

"We could talk while we walk. There are just enough clouds that we should have a beautiful sunset."

"No more walks. The beach is an unsecurable environment."

"You're kidding, right?"

"Wrong. You'd be an easy target for a sniper."

"Where wouldn't I be?"

"In areas and situations I deem secure and protected."

"My pool?"

"No problem. It's surrounded by a privacy fence. You can use the deck around the pool, but not the deck that extends beyond the fence. I'll check the other outside areas as soon as I've unpacked and see what else is off-limits."

The situation felt even more ominous than when Max

had first showed her the list with her name printed garishly across the bottom. The man who had shot Bernie Brusco in the head and strangled Mary Hancock could very well be planning her death while she stood here wondering why the chief of police didn't lust after her.

That thought not only put things in perspective but made her blood run cold. No more walks on the beach. She was a prisoner in her own home. For that matter, so was Max.

"Thanks, Max, for giving up your nights to protect me."

He stopped what he was doing and met her gaze. His green eyes took on a smoky glaze that seemed to speak to her soul. "No need to thank me. I'm here because I want to be, Callie, and I'll stay as long as you're in danger."

The frigid chill she'd felt melted away. She didn't understand Max Zirinsky at all, but she trusted him with her life. And that was good enough for now.

IF CALLIE COULDN'T WALK, she'd swim. She stepped out of her white slacks and panties and slipped the pale yellow blouse and lacy scrap of bra from her shoulders. Totally au naturel, she stood in front of the full-length mirror in her bedroom and scrutinized her figure.

The thighs and calves were good, thanks to all the walking. And the waist and abdomen? Not bad for a forty-year-old, she decided, as she let her hands press into the firm muscles of her stomach. No stretch marks since she'd never been pregnant.

No baby to cuddle and love, either, but she wasn't going there tonight, not with all the other problems she had on her plate.

She rummaged in a bureau drawer for a bathing suit and chose a light blue bikini that Mikki had talked her into buying from a snazzy little boutique in La Jolla. It probably wasn't the least seductive suit in her collection, but it was way more conservative than her birthday suit. Not that Max was likely to notice unless she wrapped herself in crime-scene tape.

She was wiggling into the bottom half of her bikini when the phone rang. Probably Mikki. She'd have a million questions when she found out Max had moved in, and Callie hadn't practiced so much as one answer yet.

She started to ignore the ring, but changed her mind when she checked the caller ID.

"Hello."

"Hi, Callie. It's Henry Lalane. I was about to hang up. Did I ring at a bad time?"

"Yes, but I can talk for a few minutes. Can I help you with something?"

"I just wanted to chat a minute."

She didn't buy that for a second, not when the district attorney had never called her before. "What is it you want to chat about?"

"Actually, I might as well just say it. Some of us were talking at Judge Craven's party yesterday, and it didn't sit well with us that you brought Max Zirinsky to the event."

"I have no idea what you mean."

"You can't expect your friends to be comfortable around Max under the circumstances."

"What circumstances would those be, Henry?"

"He's questioned some of the most upstanding men in the community as if they were suspects. He's stepped on a lot of toes with that attitude."

"Max Zirinsky is chief of police in Courage Bay. The Avenger is a dangerous killer. I don't think any of us should be concerned about toes getting stepped on."

"Nonetheless, Max has never chosen to accept an invitation to such a purely social gathering before, and his presence yesterday didn't sit too well with lots of people."

Callie had a difficult time believing Henry had made this call, especially after Mary's murder. She took a deep breath. If she wasn't so irritated with Henry Lalane right now that she couldn't think straight, she might have saved her announcement. But she was too angry to remain silent.

"I'm sorry, Henry, but I'll be bringing Max to many more social engagements."

"If you do, you should expect repercussions. And don't think you fooled anyone. We all knew why he was at the party. No one believes the two of you are actually dating."

"You're right, Henry. We're not dating. We're living together. Now if you'll excuse me, I want to get back to my lover."

She hung up the phone without waiting for a goodbye, then dropped to the edge of the bed. Either the Avenger situation had everybody so shaken that no one was the same anymore, or Henry Lalane was basically a pretentious jerk.

And now he'd be out spreading the word that Max and Callie were living together. Living together but not touching. She wondered what a man like Henry would make of that.

MAX TOOK AN ICY SHOWER, then dressed in a pair of cut-offs and a T-shirt with the Dodgers emblem emblazoned across the front. He was here, living in the same house with Callie Baker, and he would handle the situation without letting his libido take charge.

This was all business, very serious business. Determined and feeling in control, he marched out of the guest room and tromped down the stairs the same way he did at headquarters, like a bull on speed.

Only this time he stopped midway down. Callie was at the foot of the stairs, dressed in a sky-blue bikini that barely covered her nipples and showed an enticing expanse of flesh at her stomach.

His resolve melted like ice over red-hot coals. And all he could do was try not to drool while he pretended the desire coursing through him was nothing but a severe case of indigestion.

It was going to be a hell of a night.

CHAPTER NINE

MAX SAT AT THE EDGE of the pool, his bare feet dangling in the water while Callie swam laps. Her svelte body moved through the water with the grace of a dancer. By contrast, he felt awkward, a fake, like a kid playing at being a cop.

A forty-five-year-old chief of police should be able to separate his fantasies from reality, yet tonight his mind and his emotions were so tangled, he couldn't begin to find the hard edge he needed to do his job the way it should be done. Only in his dreams had he imagined himself doing sleepovers at Callie's. In his worst nightmares, he'd never imagined her the target of a mad killer.

Callie was ten years of memories, a few regrets and lots of heat thrown into the mix. He'd met her for the first time the night he'd been the best man at Tony's wedding. He'd just finished a stint with the National Guard and had endured thirty-six hours of flights, stand-bys and layovers to make it to the wedding.

Exhausted, he'd only wanted to see Tony married and find a halfway decent bed to collapse in. The idea of a noisy, boisterous Zirinsky wedding reception had had all the appeal of a torture chamber. Max had been so tired he'd fumbled when he went to hand Tony the ring. It had fallen to the carpeted aisle and bounced and rolled its way several feet before coming to rest beneath a large brass candle holder.

Some of the guests had snickered as he got down on his hands and knees to retrieve it, and Max had never felt like such a klutz. When he'd recovered the gold band, he met Callie's gaze, expecting to see disdain, since he'd spoiled her perfect ceremony. Instead she'd smiled as if they shared a private joke, and the warmth in those big brown eyes had sent his pulse racing like a schoolboy's.

From that second he'd secretly coveted his cousin's wife. Not that he'd have acted on his feelings. Like every guy with any kind of normal sex drive, he knew that lusting in your heart wasn't nearly the same as making a play for another guy's wife.

So he'd just stood by and watched Tony throw it all away. Until... Max felt his muscles tense. He couldn't go there tonight, not when Callie was probably almost as vulnerable now as she'd been that night.

After finishing her laps, she floated on her back. The water splashed around her body, gently swishing between her thighs and over her nearly bare breasts. When she floated to his side of the pool, she rolled over and swam to the edge. Grabbing his right foot for support, she tugged playfully as if she were trying to pull him in.

"You could join me." she said.

"I don't have a bathing suit with me."

"Swim without one. I won't tell."

She was teasing, but it got to him anyway. Needing to kill the stirring of arousal, he jumped up and grabbed a towel from a huge wicker basket, tossing it to her as she swung onto the ladder and climbed out of the pool.

Pickering caught the end of the towel and tried to tug it from her. Callie stooped to tussle with him, and the bikini top slipped a bit, showing mounds of soft breast. Max turned away and started back toward the house. He could only take so much.

Callie followed him, still dripping wet and smelling of chlorine and summer. "Guess if we're going to live together we should make some rules," she said. Her tone was lighter than he'd have expected under the circumstances, and he knew she was working hard not to let a frightening and tense situation overwhelm her.

The least he could do was play along. "What kind of rules do you have in mind?"

"Roomie rules, you know, like who cooks on what nights? Does the cook clean up the kitchen? Who controls the remote for the TV in the family room?"

"That's easy," he said, then made one of those male guttural noises in the back of his throat. "You woman. You cook and clean up the kitchen. Me man. Me control the remote."

"Of course. I think I read that somewhere." Callie put her finger to her cheek as if deep in thought. "I think it was in one of those self-help books on how to lose a woman in under twenty minutes."

She opened the refrigerator door and bent over to get a better look. "Someone should buy food." She pushed a carton of milk to the side so she could search behind it, then opened one of the crisper drawers. "Not a lot to choose from. We can have a BLT with cheese on toasted wheat bread or…" She opened another drawer. "Or we can order out."

"BLT sounds good to me, and I can actually fry bacon."

"Then we're in business, Chief. If you'll get the bacon started, I'll run upstairs and change into something that's not dripping all over my kitchen floor."

And something that covered more flesh, Max hoped, though that might not make a lot of difference.

"Best skillet for bacon is in the dishwasher," she said, "but it's clean."

Max found the skillet while Callie pulled the sandwich makings out of the fridge and placed them on the counter.

"I won't be but a few minutes," she said.

"Take as long as you like. Dinner is under control."

Dinner was the only thing under control. As Max peeled the slices of bacon from the slab, his mind went back to the list that had included Callie's name.

Realistically he knew it was a jump to assume the killer had typed out that list, then scribbled Callie's name on it in a very shaky hand. A jump, but not one any good detective wouldn't make, or at least consider.

The grossly misshapen letters suggested the name had been added by a person who was angry or at least on edge. But if it was the Avenger, he hadn't done anything at the party to call attention to himself. But then he wouldn't. He didn't work that way. He waited until the time was right and he had all his sick little ducks in a row.

He'd do that with Callie, too. Find the perfect time, the perfect method. And just the right opportunity. If he had any MO, it was using situations to shield himself. A mud slide. A caved roof. A crisis at City Hall. A party at Mary Hancock's house.

Max forked the bacon with a vengeance. The task of protecting Callie would be nonstop twenty-four hours a day for as long as it took to apprehend the Avenger. And there could be no mistakes.

Callie stripped out of the wet bikini. Max could pretend to have no interest in her all he wanted, but she'd seen the bulge in his shorts when she'd swam up to him in the pool. His arousal confused her all the more. If he found her attractive, why did he keep such a safe physical and emotional distance between them?

They were both divorced and had been for a long time. Both were professionals, happy and fulfilled in their chosen fields. So what was it about her that made him behave as if he were in the running for the next pope?

And why did it bother her when she had much more important matters on her mind?

Callie changed into a pair of tan shorts and a lime

green tank top, then ran a comb through her damp hair, smoothing the tangled locks.

She was about to close the door and return to the kitchen when her phone rang. She could ignore it since she wasn't on call tonight, but she had this thing about a ringing phone and junk mail. One had to be answered; the other had to be opened—just in case they were important.

"Hello."

"Dr. Baker?"

Callie recognized Gail's voice, and from the sniffing on the other end of the line, the teenager had obviously been crying. Callie seldom gave her home number to the residents at the Keller Center, preferring they go through one of the nurses or administrators at the center if they needed to talk to her. But Gail was so frightened, and she didn't seem to open up to anyone but Callie.

"What's the matter, Gail?"

"I can't stop crying."

"Are you in some kind of pain?"

"No. Well, yes, but it's in my heart."

"You mean like heartache, not chest pains."

"Right."

"Did something happen to upset you?"

"I talked to the social worker again today about adoption."

"No one will force that on you. It will be your choice."

"I know, but…" Her words were interrupted by more sniffing. "I'm a horrible person. I don't want to be a mother. Not yet. I don't know how…"

She broke into sobs again. "I don't know what to do once they're born."

"Babies are a big responsibility. Only you can decide if you're ready for it. Choosing adoption doesn't make you a horrible person."

"I called my mother today."

So there was more to this than just talking to the social worker. "What did she say?"

"I can come home after this, but I can't bring the babies. She said it's not fair to her and Daddy and my little brothers. I know she's right, but…"

But telling Gail all that on the phone wasn't fair, either. She needed her mother to put her arms around her and reassure her that she loved her, not just throw out ultimatums.

"I wish you could come see me," Gail said.

"I was just there yesterday."

"I know, but you're the only one who understands."

"I can't deal with the adoption question for you, Gail. You have to think rationally about what's best for you and the babies, and you can't do that if you don't pull yourself together."

"I know. The nurse already told me that getting upset is bad for the babies."

"And bad for you. So promise me that you'll talk to one of the counselors about this. She'll be able to help you work through the issues better than I can. You have to trust them."

"But can you come on Saturday? I know you usually come every other Saturday, but I can't wait that long."

"I'll be there, Gail, unless some type of emergency comes up. You can call me if you need to talk, but I want you to try to think of positive things between now and next Saturday."

"What positive things?"

"Your unborn babies are healthy. There haven't been any complications with the pregnancy. You're living at the Keller Center, where you'll get the best of care."

"And I'm going to throw my babies away."

"You're doing no such thing. If you decide on adoption, they'll be placed with parents who will love them and take care of them. Giving them up doesn't mean you don't love them."

"I could do it if I knew they were going to someone like you. You'd love them. You'd be a good mother."

Gail meant the comment as a compliment, but it went down like a swallow of something bitter. "Things will work out, Gail. You're a strong, smart girl, and I know you'll make good decisions. Now get some rest. You have two babies who need you to keep them healthy."

"Yes, ma'am."

Callie hung up the phone slowly, her mood altered by the phone call. Strange how a minute here and there could change a person's life so that it was never the same again. For Gail, the night she'd gotten pregnant had been one of those moments.

Callie only hoped that having her name added to a list of the Avenger's victims would not become one of those moments for her.

CALLIE AND MAX ATE their sandwiches in a cozy breakfast nook that looked out over the pool. The nook, like the rest of the house, was as snug as Callie's bikini. Not that Max usually noticed things like houses, but then he never spent much time in any. His own apartment was small, and more or less nondescript.

"I like the bright colors," Max said, glancing from a painting on the wall behind Callie to a huge red glass bowl on top of a bright yellow baker's rack.

"It's eclectic," Callie said, "but fun. Most of the furnishings and collections of art were Aunt Louise's. I inherited them along with the house, but they felt right to me, so I kept them."

"The two of you must have had a lot in common."

"Don't I wish. She was a risk-taker, quite scandalous in her day and very unlike my father, who was her brother. He and my mother were terrific parents right up until the day Dad's private jet went down in the Pacific while I was in med school. But they were both extremely conservative."

"Do you want to be scandalous?"

"It could be fun."

She met his gaze, and he could almost swear there was a challenge shining in her eyes. He wondered what she'd do if he took her up on it. Wondered if sweeping everything off the table and taking her right here and now would be scandalous enough for her.

The idea was heady, and his libido swung into gear like his old T-bird used to do when he gunned it into overdrive. Maybe when this was over, he'd do just that. Go for scandalous. Make love like there was no tomorrow.

And then wish the hell he hadn't when Callie realized there was no way a guy like him could fit in her life. She'd jump right back into her career and social circuit. He'd be back at the Bar and Grill, spending night after exciting night eating his burger with Jake the bartender, then going back to his apartment and falling asleep in his chair with police reports and tormenting memories knocking about in his mind.

Callie pushed the plate holding her half-eaten sandwich away and dabbed her mouth with her cotton napkin. "Henry Lalane called me earlier tonight."

That changed the mood fast enough. "How much earlier?"

"While I was changing into my bathing suit. I didn't mention it because I was eager to jump in the pool and get my laps in. I needed the physical exercise to help relax my nerves."

"What did he want?" Max asked.

"Seems he didn't approve of my bringing you to the Cravens' party yesterday."

"Interesting. Exactly what did he have to say?"

He listened while Callie related the details of the conversation, his cop instincts checking in. The call might not mean a thing, but coupled with Henry's appearance at Mary's the day of her drowning, it did raise a few suspicions. Not that Henry wasn't already high on Max's suspect list.

Max smiled to himself when Callie told him how she finished the conversation. He'd like to have seen Henry's face at that remark.

But if Henry knew they were living together, so would at least half of Courage Bay by tomorrow, including everybody on the police force. There would be lots of smiles and knowing looks from the guys on the force, and cracks behind his back about the chief's finally getting laid. A few of his colleagues would be smart enough to figure out what was really going on.

"What about Jerry Hawkins?" Callie asked.

"What about him?"

"Are you going to question him?"

"I thought I might pay a visit to his ex-partner's wife in Sacramento first. I'd like to talk to her before I question Jerry."

"When are you going?"

"Tuesday, I think, unless something else comes up. I can get a flight out in the morning and be back by the time you finish up at the hospital."

Callie fingered her napkin, then rested her elbows on the table and leaned in closer. "I want to go with you."

The sandwich had gone down easy, but now it balled in Max's stomach as if he'd swallowed it whole. "No way."

Her eyebrows arched. "Why not?"

"We've been over this. You're not a detective. You are not part of the investigative team."

"Because you thought getting involved would put me in danger. Well, guess what, Max. I'm there."

"We don't know that. This is all precautionary, just in case the list was the work of the Avenger."

"Precautionary or not, I'm already under official protection twenty-four hours a day. Besides, you don't have to tell his partner's wife I'm a doctor."

"I can't lie and say you're a detective."

"Then don't say anything. Just introduce me by name. She'll assume I'm a detective. Besides, you can protect me yourself that day and release my cop bodyguard for more important tasks."

Max couldn't think of any more important task, but the idea of having Callie with him was appealing, especially now that he realized that even the latest threat hadn't deterred her from sticking her beautiful nose right into the middle of the investigation.

He almost said yes, then stopped himself. If this was anyone but Callie Baker, he wouldn't be considering it. "I can't let you do this, Callie."

She started clearing the table, stacking their plates with such force it was a wonder she didn't break them. "Fine, I'll go by myself."

"I'm definitely not approving that."

"I don't need your approval. Like you said, I'm not one of your detectives. I don't work for you, and you can't order me around."

He stood and followed her to the kitchen, watching as she slid the plates beneath a spray of water from the faucet then loaded them into the dishwasher. She was one hardheaded woman. She could go to Sacramento and probably would, whether he approved it or not.

Callie was obviously starting to think like everyone else in town: Max had had eight months to find the Avenger, and he hadn't accomplished a damn thing.

"I know I haven't gotten far in catching this guy, Callie, but it's not for lack of trying."

She let the silverware she was holding slide from her fingers and clatter into the sink. "I never thought it was," she said, turning to face him. "This isn't about you, Max. Mikki's my friend, yet I'm standing by and doing nothing while she falls for a guy who could be a killer."

"You're doing it to protect her. If she suspects Hawkins and starts questioning him and it turns out he is guilty, there's no telling how he'll react."

"That doesn't make this any easier for me."

"I'm assigning a detective to dig up everything about Hawkins tomorrow. And I'm going to Sacramento myself on Tuesday. If he's guilty of anything, we'll find out and arrest him. Besides, don't you have appointments scheduled for Tuesday?"

"I have hospital business in the morning and patient appointments in the afternoon, but I can rearrange those and get another doctor to take care of rounds for me. Mikki's my friend, Max. She'd do this for me."

She kept staring at him with those beautiful eyes and

he couldn't for the life of him find a way to tell her that being a friend didn't matter, that her feelings didn't matter. But there would be one advantage to this. If Callie was with him, he knew he could keep her safe.

He took a deep breath, wondering how in the world one woman could turn him inside out with a look. "Okay, Callie. You can go, but you can't tell anyone about this, and you have to let me handle the talking once we get to Sacramento."

"Of course." She dried her hands on the dish towel, then reached over, slipped her hands in his and squeezed. "Thanks, Max."

The heat of her touch shot through him, and he had trouble swallowing until she let go and went back to the dishes. Max walked to the breakfast nook, gathered the place mats and two tea glasses they'd left behind.

The scandalous thoughts he'd entertained earlier returned, burning hot inside him as he stood over the table and pictured Callie on top of it, and him…

Pickering nudged his nose against Max's leg and Max let the image fade. "You're right, Pickering,' he said, patting the retriever on the head. "I am a complete fool."

CALLIE RAN ALONG THE SAND, close enough to the surf that each wave washed over her feet and splashed up her legs. The sun was high in the sky, yet she was the only one on the lonely stretch of beach. Just her, Pickering and the seagulls that squawked overhead.

Then, as if from nowhere, she heard footsteps behind

her. Someone was running even faster than she was and gaining on her. She turned and saw the runner just as thunder crashed and lightning streaked across a sky that had suddenly grown dark and full of black, tumultuous clouds.

"Take the babies, Callie. You have to take the babies."

It was Gail, pregnant, her stomach bulging beneath her T-shirt, but she had a baby in each arm. The infants were smiling and holding their chubby little arms out to Callie.

"You have to take them. If you don't, I have to throw them into the surf."

Callie ran all the harder, only now it seemed as if she'd been running for days. Her legs ached and stabs of pain shot through her side. The thunder cracked again, and the rain started falling, feeling like needle pricks as the wind pushed it into her face.

She turned around to check on the babies, but now it was a man behind her, closing in fast. His bare feet flew along the sand, and he was waving something at her. She blinked and tried to see through the sheets of rain.

Oh, no! He was waving a gun. The killer. The Avenger. But he had no face!

Callie fell to her knees, unable to run any further. He was going to kill her.

The barrel of the pistol was against her temple now. She heard the click of the hammer and the man's husky breathing.

She tried to scream, but the water rushed into her

lungs, choking her. In a frenzy she beat her fists against the sand. It was all over. There was no way to escape.

And then Callie woke. She was sitting straight up in bed, her arms and legs tangled in the sheet and light blanket. It was a nightmare. Gail. The babies. The face-less killer. All a horrifying, bizarre nightmare.

But it had seemed so real. Even now her heart was pounding in her chest. She sucked in a deep breath and listened to see if the rain and thunder had been real. But the night was quiet, except for a low, rhythmic noise from down the hallway.

Max Zirinsky. She lay in the darkness, listening to the almost hypnotic sound of his snoring, and thought she'd never heard anything so beautiful.

It was terrific to know that a man like Max was on her side. Still shivering from the fear that had gripped her only moments ago, she tried to imagine what it would be like to crawl into bed beside him and have him hold her in those strong arms.

With any luck, she'd find out one day. But tonight, she'd settle for just knowing he was there.

MAX SPENT THE GREATER PART of Monday morning at the catering service for Mary Hancock's party. He'd talked to every single person who'd worked at that party, and no one had seen anything suspicious. But then the staff had been extremely busy, and most said there were so many people around that they'd probably never have noticed someone removing and then replacing a few canapés.

Batting zero again. No surprise, but he kept hoping. Sooner or later the killer would make a mistake. It was amazing that he hadn't already, at least not one that Max or the other detectives who'd been handling the case had discovered.

The man was thorough, and seemed to have organized his attacks down to the most minute detail. Yet he'd been able to switch gears quickly enough when his first attempt on Bernie's life had gone awry.

If he was a member of Courage Bay's social elite, the kind of person who'd have been invited to Mary's fundraiser and the Cravens' garden party, then he had to know that when his identity was discovered, life as he knew it would be over.

Max was almost back to headquarters when his cell phone rang. Forensics. He hardly dared hope they'd have some news.

"What's up?" he asked, instead of bothering with a hello.

"That list you dropped off yesterday."

"Yeah?"

"We found prints that didn't belong to Mrs. Craven."

"Anyone who was in the database?" Max practically held his breath as he waited for the answer.

"Oh, yeah, he's in the database. All the employees in his office are. The prints belong to district attorney Henry Lalane."

CHAPTER TEN

MAX HAD WORKED CLOSELY with Henry Lalane on lots of cases. Lalane hadn't always liked the way Max's CSI team or his detectives did their jobs, and Max hadn't always approved of how Lalane handled the trials or who he allowed to plea bargain. Nonetheless, there had been a mutual respect between them.

Max's mind drifted back to the first name on the list Marjorie had found. Dr. George Yube. At one time Yube had been a respected surgeon, chief of surgery at Courage Bay Hospital. And then his past had caught up with him.

While moonlighting in the hospital's E.R. during his first year of surgery residency, Yube had partied too hard, shown up for work under the influence and botched an emergency delivery, resulting in a dead baby.

Figuring he'd be sued and likely kicked out of the residency program, Yube had switched the dead infant for another baby in the hospital nursery. In the process of finding an infant of the same weight, he'd removed three babies from their incubators. After weighing and measuring them, he'd unwittingly returned them to the wrong incubators, and separated twin girls in the process.

Years later Yube was charged with attempted homicide after he tried to kill Lauren Conway, one of the twins, when she began to uncover the truth of her parentage.

But that wasn't the end of the story. On the day Yube's attorney, Faith Lawton, got the doctor released on a technicality, Yube was fatally shot by a sniper while leaving the courthouse. Faith and Adam Guthrie, Max's chief of detectives, had both been standing within inches of Yube.

Eventually the evidence had indicated Felix Moody as the shooter and Adam Guthrie as the assumed target. But before Moody was arrested, he took Faith hostage in her own office. Guthrie had gone to her rescue and Moody had been killed in the showdown. At that point, the case had been closed, and Faith and Adam had gotten married. A hell of a terrific ending to a bad situation.

Moody had never admitted to being the sniper who'd killed Yube, yet the evidence against him was far too convincing to be circumstantial. So if Yube had been killed by the Avenger, then the Avenger had manipulated the evidence and set Moody up to take the rap, which made this case against the Avenger even more convoluted.

Max had talked briefly with Adam this morning. He didn't have any additional insight into the case and had offered to come back to the city, but Max had told him to stay put. The terrorist training seminar was too vital to blow off unless absolutely necessary. Besides, Max had the leads covered and was anxious to talk to Henry Lalane face-to-face.

As district attorney, Lalane would have been fully aware of the technicality glitch in Dr. Yube's trial and would have known that a decision was likely coming down that day. But even if Lalane had decided to take justice in his own hands, why had he started with George Yube?

The baby's switch had been committed thirty years ago, and was far removed from the type of criminal incident that had claimed the life of Henry's daughter. Yube's attempt on Lauren Conway's life had been thwarted, and the only miscarriage of justice in Henry's daughter's death was that the rotten coward who'd shot her had never been identified.

Still, Max would have to keep an open mind. If he'd learned anything at all during his years in law enforcement, it was to expect the unexpected. And the unexpected was what he planned to hit Henry Lalane with this morning.

That's why he hadn't called first. He wanted to be standing in front of Lalane and scrutinizing his body language, facial expression and even the look in his eyes when Max asked him about the incriminating sheet of paper that held his fingerprints.

THE DISTRICT ATTORNEY'S office was on the fifth floor of a gray brick building two blocks from the courthouse. Max had seen Henry hundreds of times before, but he found himself sizing up the lawyer the way he would someone he'd never met before.

Henry was in his early fifties and had the look of a man who'd lived with success all his life. He had for most of it. He'd married Janice as soon as he'd finished law school and had moved to Courage Bay, where her family was firmly entrenched in the financial, social and cultural life of the city.

He'd gained a reputation early on as a dynamic and effective trial lawyer, and once he'd been hired to work as a prosecutor for the D.A.'s office, it was only a short jump to the position of district attorney itself.

Henry leaned back in his chair and stared at Max, the look in his gray eyes guarded, though he managed a welcoming smile. "Sorry to keep you waiting," Henry said. "I was in a time-critical meeting with a defense attorney whose client wants to plea bargain. Actually, I have to get back to it quickly, but my secretary said this was important."

Max had said urgent rather than important, but no reason to swat at flies in a nest of wasps. "I appreciate your time." That was all the apology he was making. If it turned out Henry was guilty of murder, time was all the guy would have, years of it, spent behind bars.

"So, what can I help you with?" Henry asked.

Max had no intention of beating around the bush with this. Henry would see through any interrogation tactics anyway. Like all good attorneys, he was a master at asking leading questions himself.

The note with the fingerprints was being checked by a handwriting analysis expert, but Max had a copy in his shirt pocket. He took it out and handed it to the district attorney. "Have you seen this before?"

Henry unfolded the note and studied it. His expression definitely changed, but either the guy was totally innocent or he was a hell of an actor. He muttered a few curses.

"Where did you get this?" he asked.

"Someone found it on the Cravens' property after Saturday's party."

"What kind of sick bastard would add Callie Baker's name to the victim list?"

"That's what I intend to find out. Are you saying you've never seen this slip of paper before?"

"Of course not." Henry looked back at the note. "Do you think it's possible the Avenger wrote this note and that Callie actually is a target?"

"I think it's a possibility."

"Sonofabitch! Guess I owe you and Callie an apology, Max. I thought your presence at the party would create unnecessary fear among the guests, but I was wrong. If the Avenger was there, the fear was warranted."

Max found it difficult to stay seated. He preferred standing when he questioned suspects, but he wanted to play this low-key. He'd make no accusations. Wasn't going to read Henry his rights or come at him heavy-handed. Not yet, anyway.

The D.A. stared down at the note. He tapped the first name on the list with his index finger. "Why is Dr. Yube's name on this list? Felix Moody killed him. We know Moody's not the Avenger. He's dead." He reached across the desk to hand the note back to Max.

"I was hoping you could tell me why Dr. Yube's name is on the list," Max said, keeping his voice low and steady.

"Don't have a clue. Now if you'll excuse me, I need to get back to the meeting I was in."

"I think the meeting better wait, Henry."

Henry met Max's steady gaze. "You want to tell me what this visit is really about?"

"The note I showed you is just a copy. The original was fingerprinted. Your prints are on it."

Veins popped out in Henry's neck and forehead as if he were about to explode. "What did you say?"

"Your prints were on the list. I felt sure you'd have an explanation for that."

Henry jumped up from his seat, sending his desk chair rolling across the floor to crash into the book-shelves behind his desk. "There has to be some mistake. There's no way my prints could be on a victim list that included Callie Baker's name."

Max didn't respond. He just let Lalane roar and pace from the desk to the window and back again.

"I've never seen that list before today, Max, not even before Callie's name was added. If I had, I'd have noticed Dr. Yube's name on there and remembered."

Max merely nodded.

"I swear I never saw that list, so if my prints were on it, they had to have gotten there before the names were typed on the paper." Henry stopped pacing and put his hands out, palms up. "That's it. Some sonofabitch is trying to frame me. Either the Avenger or just someone who has it in for me."

If that was the case, the note should have been planted where someone was certain to find it, not left to blow around the property and almost over the edge of the cliff. Unless Marjorie Craven had lied about where she'd found the note.

"I don't suppose you'd have any objections to taking a lie detector test," Max said, "just to help clear this up."

Henry started to pace again, then dropped back into his chair. "I have plenty of objections, none of them associated with guilt."

"Want to explain?"

"Sure. You know how I feel about Bernie Brusco. Someone asks me if I think he got what he deserved, I have to say yes. If I don't, the detector's going to say I'm lying. I think he got exactly what he deserved, and so did Deeb and Esposito and all the other of the Avenger's victims except Mary Hancock, but that doesn't mean I killed them."

"As long as you tell the truth, it shouldn't affect the test results."

"Unless this stuff leaks out. I don't believe what the Avenger's done is right, but I can see why he did it. The system is screwed. It's about money and power and who's got the best attorney. Justice isn't only blind, it's crippled and on its way to becoming totally impotent."

"I can't overlook the fact that your fingerprints are on an incriminating piece of evidence."

"It's a list, Max. Not a murder weapon. I didn't write out that list, but even if I had, there are no laws against making lists. I'm innocent, Max. You must know that."

"All I know is I've got an Avenger out there killing citizens of Courage Bay, and if I don't stop him, he's going to kill again."

But Max knew he wouldn't get any more information out of Henry right now, so he might as well let the D.A. return to his meeting. Max had a little more investigating to do before he brought Henry to headquarters for official questioning. In the meantime, he'd have the attorney tailed 24/7.

His first lead. Max wasn't about to blow it off, no matter how much Lalane protested. But the truth was, Max had a hunch that Henry was every bit as innocent as he proclaimed. Which meant the fingerprints were one more mystery in the most labyrinthine plot Max had seen in his twenty-two years in law enforcement.

The Avenger, whoever he was, was intelligent, analytical and vindictive, and drew a deadly aim. If the list belonged to him, he wanted Callie dead.

CALLIE WOULD HAVE LOVED to avoid Mikki completely today, but unfortunately that was not an option. Mikki stopped by Callie's office at one-thirty, a half hour before either had an afternoon appointment scheduled. Callie had sent her police guard cum resident to the next room so that she could have a few minutes of privacy during her lunch break.

"What a morning," Mikki said, dropping into a chair opposite Callie, who sat munching a turkey and Swiss sandwich while she perused a patient chart.

"Major problems?" Callie asked.

"A run on injection-phobic kids. Real screamers. I was afraid Dr. Bisby was going to come over and accuse me of torturing children. No one ever screams in his examining rooms."

"He's a rheumatologist. His patients are older."

"Where did I go wrong?"

"You wouldn't be happy anywhere but with your little ones." Callie took a swig of bottled water. "Speaking of little ones, I had a call from Gail Lodestrum last night."

"No problems with the pregnancy, I hope."

"No. She's feeling guilty because she doesn't want to keep the babies."

"Poor kid. She's not much more than a baby herself. But then the thought of having twins would frighten me, and I'm practically twice her age. Adoption does seem a viable option for her, especially since she has no support from her family or the biological father."

"She talked to her mother yesterday. They'll take her back, but not the twins. That sent Gail on a crying jag that wouldn't stop."

"Then you think she wants to keep the babies?"

"No. I figure it's more guilt than desire for motherhood that makes her afraid of adoption."

"Hopefully the social workers can help her work through this. Keller Center has some of the best."

"I encouraged her to talk to them. I think she was in a slightly better mood when she hung up."

Mikki reached in the pocket of her lab coat and pulled out one of the brightly colored lollipops she used to reward her young patients. She tossed it to Callie. "Good job, Doc."

"Maybe too good. Gail thinks I'd make a good mother for her twins."

Mikki nodded. "Might not be such a bad idea."

"Maybe you have spent too much time with screamers," Callie said. "You seem to have completely lost your senses."

"Why? You'd make a great mother."

"With the hours I keep, I'd have to make an appointment to see my kids."

"You work too hard, anyway. It's probably time you slowed down. Get a husband, a couple of kids, one of those soccer mom SUVs."

"I don't think you can adopt husbands."

"You probably can find one on eBay, but I suggest you look yourself. I'm thinking mid-forties, fairly tall, some muscles, dark hair, piercing green eyes. Your basic chief of police type."

This was the perfect opening to throw out the fact that she and Max were living together, Callie figured. If Mikki heard it from someone else first, she'd be crushed. But telling her meant that Callie would have to lie about the circumstances, and lying to Mikki would be difficult, if not downright impossible. Mikki knew her far too well.

Callie stalled. "So, what exciting things do you have on your calendar this week?" she asked.

"Jerry's coming over tonight and cooking dinner for me."

Cold dread filled Callie. "Dating on a work night? That's not like you."

"I know. This is different." Mikki uncrossed her legs and wagged a finger at Callie. "Don't look at me that way. I know I've said the same thing before, but this time it really is different."

"How so?" Callie asked.

"The way I feel when I'm with him. My heart actually sings."

"Is he more fun than your hot firemen?" Callie hoped the answer would be no and give Mikki food for thought.

"Not always." Mikki leaned back and grew pensive. "He can be lots of fun, but he's quiet sometimes, too. He's a little mysterious. That's probably part of the intrigue."

Callie slid her hands up and down her arms, trying to calm the fears that were so potent they had raised the hairs on the back of her neck. She'd follow Max's advice one more day, but if she still felt this way after tomorrow's visit to Sacramento, she would have to voice her concerns to Mikki. Not that she was certain Mikki would listen.

"What about you and Max?" Mikki asked. "Still playing the dating game?"

The question was blatant. There was no avoiding the issue now. Callie sucked in a deep breath and exhaled slowly. "We're living together."

Mikki came out of her chair as if she'd been shot from a cannon. She shoved some files out of the way and perched on the edge of Callie's desk. "And you waited until now to tell me? Come on. Give, girlfriend. What bought this on?"

"We... He... It's..."

She couldn't do it. It was bad enough she wasn't leveling with Mikki about her suspicions about Jerry. She couldn't lie about her relationship with Max, but neither could she tell her friend about the list. That was classified information.

"It's police business," Callie said. "This way I can accompany Max to various social functions without—he hopes—arousing suspicion."

"Then he still believes the Avenger was a guest at Mary's party the other night?"

"He believes it's possible. And it's better if everyone thinks we're a couple, so you can't say a word about our real arrangement to anyone, not even Jerry Hawkins." Especially not Jerry Hawkins.

"Jerry wouldn't repeat the info if I asked him not to."

"No one, Mikki. I need your promise on that."

"Okay. I promise. It's far more titillating to think of you two as lovers anyway."

"You can think it. So can the rest of the town. But we're not."

"Well, not yet, but if you two start sleeping in the same house together, you will be soon. The kind of heat you two put out can't be cooled down with a glass of wine or a dip in that pool of yours."

Callie tried to block the images that sneaked into her mind at Mikki's words, but she wasn't entirely successful. She felt a slow burn creep across her skin and knew she had to be blushing. For once, Mikki didn't seem to notice.

Mikki pushed up her sleeve and glanced at her animated Minnie Mouse watch, which her patients loved. "Gotta go. The screamers' moms get restless if we run late."

Callie wrapped the rest of her sandwich in her paper napkin, tossed it into the trash can by her desk, then stood and walked to the door with Mikki. The warnings she ached to give formed a lump in her throat. "Take care," she said.

"You, too. Stay safe." Mikki reached over and gave one of Callie's hands an unexpected squeeze, as if she sensed Callie's uneasiness. "And wear something sexy tonight. Like talcum powder and a smile."

Callie stood in the doorway as Mikki walked past the examining room to the exit. Apprehension and fantasy. Strange that they could coexist, yet both were careening around inside her right now. There was no way she could think of Max without feeling the tantalizing heat of desire. No way to think of the Avenger without experiencing the pangs of fear, for Mikki, for herself and for all of Courage Bay.

MAX PICKED CALLIE UP from her hospital rounds at six-thirty, but explained that he'd been out of his office most of the afternoon and had to make a quick stop at police headquarters before they drove back to her house. It was Callie's first time in Max's office and she was intrigued by the room's setup, especially the wall map dedicated to the actions of the Avenger.

"Do the red pins indicate areas where the Avenger's struck?" she asked, realizing it was the first time she'd seen a city map with this much detail.

"Yeah. As you can see, there's no real pattern as to location."

"I don't suppose you have any more evidence on whether or not Dr. Yube was one of the Avenger's victims."

"Not yet," Max said. He walked away from the map and started gathering files from his desk and shoving them into a soft leather briefcase. "We did make progress today, though."

Callie forgot the map and hurriedly crossed the room. "What kind of progress?"

"Henry Lalane's fingerprints on the paper Marjorie Craven found."

Callie took a few steps backward and dropped into a chair, her legs suddenly too weak to support her. "Henry Lalane." The information shifted around in her mind as if searching for a place to fit. There was none. "I know he's an avid crusader to get guns and drugs off the street, but I can't see him going around killing people. I doubt he even owns a gun."

Max turned and took her hands. His felt hot, which meant hers were probably icy cold.

"Is there anyone you actually know that you do think capable of murder, Callie?"

She swallowed hard and thought about the question as honestly as she could. "No. Do you think that's why I've had such strong suspicions about Jerry Hawkins, because he's the only guest at Mary's party I don't know well?"

"It could be. You know what a difficult time Mary had believing Bernie Brusco was involved in drug trafficking."

"Yes, but she was thinking of marrying him." Callie tried to think of Henry strangling Mary and tossing her into her pool. The image wouldn't gel. Yet his prints were on the note. "Did you confront Henry?"

"Yeah."

Max dropped her hands, then filled her in on his meeting with the district attorney. She wasn't sure she was officially supposed to know all of this, but was glad Max trusted her enough to tell her.

"Are you still flying to Sacramento tomorrow?" she asked. With the evidence against Henry, Callie figured he might be ready to forget Jerry Hawkins.

"Thanks for mentioning that. I need to take the reservation info." He shuffled through some more papers on his desk, then found what he was looking for.

"Why don't you let me handle those, Max?"

"You got it." He handed the reservation printouts to her, then crossed the room and turned off the light in his office.

They walked out together, and she felt a strange bonding with him, different from the physical attraction she usually felt. This felt stronger in some way, as if they were a team, or a real couple. Now they were going home together. Only he'd sleep in one bed and she'd sleep in another.

Their hands brushed as they left the building, and Callie felt the familiar warm tingle dance along her nerve endings, then grow hot in the sensitive area between her thighs.

Mikki had predicted that if they spent too much time together, the heat of desire would consume them. Callie was already there.

HE SAT IN HIS CAR, watching Callie Baker and Max Zirinsky walk out of police headquarters together. The chief of police was manipulating the brilliant doctor and she didn't even know it. Too bad. Her naïveté was a fatal mistake.

He didn't want to kill her. But like Mary, Callie knew too much. She hadn't put the pieces together yet, but now that she was hanging out with Max, it wouldn't be long before she did.

He'd kill Callie, then he'd kill the others, the ones whose names had not been typed on the list. The list with Henry's fingerprints all over it.

He hadn't intended to frame Henry, but it was lucky that he'd typed the list on a piece of scrap paper he'd happened to pick up from Henry's desk.

At least now the suspicion was averted from him for the time being. Now he could focus on completing his mission.

A man had to do something with his life before he died, something that made a difference. His mission would be his legacy, a way to right any wrongs he might have done. And he had to stop Callie before she sabotaged his work.

CHAPTER ELEVEN

MAX HAD STOPPED at the neighborhood market on the way home. Callie had shopped at the same market hundreds of times before, yet tonight the grocery shopping seemed more like an intimate adventure than the routine chore it usually was. They'd walked the well-stocked aisles together. Chosen steaks for the grill, perused the produce department for salad makings and chosen a crusty bread flavored with herbs and sun-dried tomatoes. Max had thrown a six-pack of beer into the basket and a bag of pistachios. Callie had selected a couple of peaches and a ripe cantaloupe.

They'd laughed and talked while they shopped, and it had struck Callie that they were at the same time both new and old. Familiar, yet unfamiliar. Comfortable, yet tense with sexual undertones and the omniscient hint of danger, reminding them of the reason for being together.

At least it seemed that way to her. Max was impossible to read. He gave no indication that he was experiencing the kind of slow burn that she was.

They'd finished dinner now and were sitting in the

living area. She was sipping a glass of red wine. Max had had a beer, but he'd finished it quickly and was sitting forward in the overstuffed armchair, studying some files spread out on the hassock in front of him. Callie walked over and perched on the arm of his chair.

"Why do you have a file on Leo Garapedian?" she asked, noting the name on the tab. "Is he in on the investigation?"

"No." Max scratched his chin and the stubble that now shadowed it. "He's just one of the people I've had to consider when searching for suspects."

"But he was your chief of detectives."

"And a damn good one."

"Then how can you even imagine he might be guilty of vigilante crimes?"

"I'm a cop. It's not a matter of imagining. Unlike the judicial system, we think of everyone as a suspect until they're proven innocent."

"You're not a cop. You're the chief of police."

"That's only a title. Deep down I'm a cop. Always will be."

"Wouldn't the same be true of Leo Garapedian?"

"I hope so. But even good cops sometimes become jaded. They bust their butts to get the criminals off the streets. Then some judge or jury says they asked a question the wrong way or stubbed their toe on somebody's rights, and the perp goes free. But I don't really suspect Leo. He's quick to anger when someone walks on a technicality, but he wasn't involved in the hostage situation at City Hall and I don't have any information to place him in the area of the other murders."

"Did you question Leo about alibis?" she asked, certain that would have made Leo furious.

"Not directly. But a good detective has other ways of finding out where a man was on any given day."

"Do you have any information that links the people involved in the hostage-taking situation with the other murders?"

"Nothing, and timing is tricky on some of the deaths. For example with Deeb, the condition of the body after the mud slide made it impossible to get an exact time of death." Max closed the file and leaned back in his chair. "I'm beginning to think you really are after my job."

"No, you can have your killers. Diseases can be just as deadly, but most are far more predictable." She twisted the gold and ruby ring on her right hand, her mind still toying with the facts even though Max had closed the file.

"I keep thinking about Lorna Sinke's murder. If she wasn't killed by the Avenger, wouldn't that make the list some silly hoax as well?"

"But we don't know for sure that Lorna wasn't another Avenger victim."

"And then there's Henry Lalane," she said, still shocked that he was now a suspect. "If he's telling the truth about not writing the note, how can his fingerprints be on it?"

Max shoved a wayward lock of hair back from his forehead, then rubbed his neck as if he were trying to loosen kinks. "Another of the questions I don't have an answer for."

Max moved one foot to the corner of the hassock. The jarring movement caused a slip of paper to fall to the floor. Callie reached and picked it up. It was a copy of the list with Callie's name scribbled across the bottom. The letters seemed to jump from the page and the danger seemed all the more real. She let the paper drop through her fingers and float back to the carpet, but she couldn't stop the shudder that rocked though her.

"Don't let it get to you," Max said.

"Easier said than done." She stood and walked to the window, staring out into the darkness. Max's footfalls fell silently on the thick carpet, but Callie sensed his movement toward her and felt an almost imperceptible quickening of her pulse.

"You're safe, Callie, no matter who put your name on that list."

"I know, but when I look at that note, it's as if I feel his hate."

"It's not your doing. It's his own sickness that's festering inside him."

She swallowed hard, now keenly aware of Max's nearness. He was standing so close she could feel his breath on the back of her neck. Close, but not touching.

Finally she turned and slowly lifted her gaze, afraid that if he saw her need, he'd back away. His own gaze was intense, his deep green eyes so piercing she felt as if he were looking straight through her, that he could see her thoughts and feelings.

"Oh, Callie." Her name sounded ragged on his tongue. Almost pleading. He leaned in closer, his mouth inches from hers, his musky scent filling her senses like an aphrodisiac.

He was going to kiss her. Oh, please let him do it before she threw herself at him. Her heart drummed inside her chest, then seemed to stop beating altogether when his lips touched hers.

The kiss was hunger and desire and emotional release. The kiss was Max. Fierce. Unbridled. Primal. She didn't know or care what it meant other than that Max was as hungry for her as she was for him.

And then it was over.

Max backed away without a word, but she could see the flexed muscles in his arms and the white knuckles of his clenched fists before he released them and shoved his hands into his pockets.

He walked into the kitchen, opened his second beer of the evening and returned to his chair and his notes as if nothing had happened between them. Only the kiss *had* happened, and the air between them was as charged as a lighted stick of dynamite.

They were adults. They couldn't go on like this. *She* couldn't go on like this.

Pushed to her emotional limits, Callie crossed the room, scooped up his files and dropped them to the floor. He merely stared as she slid onto the hassock, her feet resting between it and his chair, her legs sliding between his.

"Are you going to do this every eight years, Max?"

He stared at her for long moments, his expression unreadable except for the smoky desire that haunted his eyes. "I don't know what you're talking about."

"The kiss, Max. I'm talking about the kiss."

He shrugged his shoulders but looked away. "It was a mistake. I shouldn't have kissed you."

"But you did. Kissed me senseless the same way you did eight years ago. You walked away then, too, but this time it can't be about Tony."

Placing his hands on her shoulders, he let his thumbs ride the tight lines of her neck before finally meeting her gaze. "It was never about Tony, Callie."

"Then what?"

He hesitated, as if searching for the right response. "Timing."

Timing. That might be an answer for him, but it meant nothing to her. "What kind of timing are you looking for, Max? I didn't plan to find out my husband was cheating on me, and I damn sure didn't plan to have a killer make me one of his targets. So just what kind of timing do you want?"

Need. Hurt. Anger. Frustration. Dread. The emotions were so tangled inside her she couldn't separate them.

Max dropped his hands from her shoulders and let them slide down her arms. "I don't want to hurt you,

Callie. Believe me, that's the last thing I want to do. But you're vulnerable now, the same as you were the night you ended the marriage with Tony. It's natural for you to reach out to me, but…" He took a deep breath and exhaled slowly. "I'm here to protect you, not to take advantage of you."

"And you think that's all there is to my feelings for you? You think I could kiss any man who stepped into my life and offered me protection the way I kissed you?"

"No. Of course not. I didn't meant that." He stood up and paced the room before finally dropping to the hassock beside her. "I want to make love to you, Callie Baker. I want it so badly that I can barely think straight. That's the problem. If I give into the desire, I'll never be able to keep a clear head. And right now I have to make your safety and stopping the Avenger before he kills again my top priority."

She had no argument for that. Making love wouldn't be the end all. She knew that. Breathtaking sex never satisfied as much as it whet the appetite for more. Still, she'd never wanted a man more than she wanted Max right now. And she was certain it had nothing to do with her vulnerability.

"I can live with that," she said, "but I have one request, Max."

"Anything."

"When this is over, I want to make love with you. No

holds barred. Then we'll either get it out of our system once and for all or find out that we can't."

He opened his mouth, but nothing came out, so he closed it again.

She took that for a yes.

MAX'S BODY WAS ROCK HARD as he watched Callie walk up the stairs to her bedroom. He was still hiding inside the tough cop exterior, but the tightly coiled sexual drive he felt scared him half to death.

He hadn't exactly lied to Callie, but he hadn't told the full truth, either. He was not even certain he knew what the truth was. He'd loved her for so long now, it seemed like part of his existence—like eating, or sleeping, or breathing. But he'd also come to accept that they'd never be together.

They'd make love when this was over, if that was still what Callie wanted. They might even try to mesh their lives together. But the pieces would never fit. His edges were jagged and rough; hers were smooth and polished. He didn't make small talk, didn't understand the opera or get excited over some guy in tights bouncing across a stage. He'd as soon wear a straitjacket as get dressed up in a tux with tails. Any way you tied it up and let it dangle, he simply wouldn't fit in her life.

She'd realize that and walk away. He'd eat and sleep alone again. But he'd remember how she'd looked in the morning all sleepy-eyed and disheveled, remember how her hair smelled and the scent of perfume she wore, remember how she tasted and how she felt lying naked next to him in the bed they'd shared.

He'd remember it and ache for her every day for the rest of his life.

MIKKI RAN HER TONGUE over her top lip, picking up the dab of sweet cream that had missed her mouth. "Don't be so stingy," she said. "I like a mouthful."

"Gluttony is not ladylike," Jerry announced in a scolding tone even as he scooped up extra hot fudge sauce from the sundae they were sharing. He poked the spoon between her open lips and she closed her mouth over the creamy concoction of ice cream, fudge syrup, nuts and whipped cream.

"Now you're drooling," he admonished. He leaned in closer and kissed the smeared chocolate from her lips. "What nasty habit will you demonstrate next?"

"Wouldn't you like to know?" She took the spoon from him and fed him a bite.

"Mmm. That's almost as good as…"

He let the sentence die on his lips, though his seductive smile said it all. She set the dish of ice cream on the coffee table and scooted closer. "As good as this?" She gave him a playful kiss, teasing with her tongue, then pulling away.

"Not nearly as good as that."

They were making out like teenagers in heat, and Mikki was loving every second of it. Not just because of the teasing. She was used to that. Teasing and playful flirting were her trademarks.

But it was different with Jerry. He didn't just make her laugh. He made her heart race and made her feel as if she were glowing inside. Part of it was that he was so damn sexy with his bronzed skin, manly physique and boyish smile that tilted up on one side and sort of puckered on the other. Mostly it was some abstract quality she couldn't begin to describe.

He kissed her again, then thrust his fingers in her hair. "If I don't get out of here soon, I may not leave at all."

"Now, that's a thought."

He raised an eyebrow. "You are wanton, lady."

"Do you have a problem with that?"

"I don't know. I guess I'd have to hang around awhile and see."

"Great idea, except that you live in Sacramento."

"I'm not there now."

"Why are you in Courage Bay?" she asked, suddenly remembering Callie's remark that he was recovering from an injury.

"Fate. And an extended vacation."

But his mood seemed to change in an instant. His eyes took on a shadowed look and she had the bizarre feeling that he was crawling back inside himself. Mikki was daunted, but only for a few seconds. "Did I say something wrong?"

"No. I just have a lot on my mind."

"Does it have to do with Bernie Brusco?"

"Whatever gave you that idea?"

"I don't know. The rest of the city seems to be totally

wrapped up in the Avenger's actions. I thought you might be, too."

"Bernie's not worth the brain cells needed to give him a second thought. The world is definitely a better place without him and all the other swine who make their living destroying lives."

His tone was harsh, in stark contrast to the playful spirit he'd exhibited a few moments earlier. For a man who could be so witty and tender, he definitely had his darker moods.

"Let's not talk about Bernie tonight," he said. "Besides, our ice cream is melting."

"I don't want any more ice cream," she whispered, scooting closer and putting her mouth to his ear.

He turned and trailed a finger down her face, slowly, sensually, from her forehead to her lips. "You need some sleep."

"No." She caught his finger between her lips, sucking and tasting, before she released it. "What I need is you, Jerry Hawkins. In my bed. All night long."

She leaned her head against his broad shoulder and he rested his chin on her hair. "You're probably making a big mistake inviting me for a sleepover," he said.

"Why? Are you dangerous?"

"Guess you'll have to wait and see."

But danger was far from her mind as he swooped her up in his arms and carried her to the bedroom.

CALLIE AND MAX ARRIVED at the airport ninety minutes before their scheduled departure. For once the security check went smoothly with only minor delays, and they headed toward the gate with an hour to spare.

"Do you want breakfast?" Max asked as they passed a café that smelled of bacon and spicy sausage.

"No, but coffee would be good."

She fell in line behind Max, then spotted Lawrence Craven sitting by himself at one of the tables, munching on a bagel and reading the morning newspaper. She touched Max's arm. "Do you mind getting mine while I go say hello to Judge Craven? He's sitting by the window."

"No problem. Black, as usual?"

"No. Make this one café au lait."

Max glanced over at the judge. "Looks as if he's traveling alone. Must be business."

"He was alone the last time I ran into him at the airport," Callie said. "Marjorie has so many volunteer projects, she probably doesn't have time to join him on short business trips."

Max turned back to the counter and Callie walked toward the judge.

Lawrence Craven was a handsome man, Callie thought, with salt and pepper hair and a lithe build. He had a way of looking at a person as if he were your best friend and listening to what you had to say was the most important thing in the world to him. That had to be disconcerting for convicted criminals when they stood before him, waiting for their sentence to be handed out.

"Hello, Lawrence."

He looked up from his paper and smiled. "Callie Baker. Nice to see you again. You look lovely, as always."

"Thanks."

He stood and pulled out a chair for her, the perfect gentleman. "Are you traveling for business or pleasure?" he asked as she settled in the seat.

Neither, but she wasn't about to explain. "Max and I are flying to Sacramento for the day."

"Then the two of you really are a couple?"

"Yes."

"I must say that surprises me. I think it's great, though. Max is a good man. Rough around the edges, but that has little to do with character."

"I'm glad you approve."

"I do. Some people were bent out of shape when you brought Max to the garden party, but my matchmaker Marjorie was delighted. She thinks Max is…" He struck a thinker's pose. "Virile. Yes, that's it. She said our chief of police is quite virile."

He folded his paper and pushed it to the edge of the table as Max joined them with coffee. "I wish I could stay and visit with you two," the judge said, "but my plane for San Francisco boards in about ten minutes."

"Well, at least we got to say hello." Max sat down as the judge rose. "How's your wife?"

"Worried." The judge picked up his briefcase from the extra chair but made no other move toward leaving. "Actually, I'm worried about her." His gaze went from Max to Callie.

"You can say what's on your mind," Max said. "Callie knows about the list your wife found."

"I wish she'd never found it." Stress lines contorted the judge's face. "She's obsessing over it and Mary's death. I'm encouraging her to go to her sister's in Seattle for a few days to get away from all of this. I'll insist on it if the newshounds start swarming the house with their endless questions."

"We're not releasing information about the list to the press," Max told him.

"Good, but that doesn't mean it won't leak out. Sooner or later, information like that always does."

"Well, I hope you have a good flight today," Max said, obviously uncomfortable discussing an ongoing case. "Will you be in San Francisco long?"

"Just for the day. I'm visiting a friend."

"Good day for it, I guess."

"As good as any. He has an inoperable brain tumor. I try to see him once a month, but I never know when our visit will be the last one." He pushed up his sleeve and glanced at his Rolex. "I really must go. Enjoy your day."

Max toyed with the stir stick, then took a quick sip of coffee. "I need to make a phone call. I'll be where I can see you, so stay right here until I get back."

Obviously the phone call was private, so Callie sat quietly, enjoying her coffee and contemplating the day ahead of them. By noon, they'd be at the home of Jerry Hawkins' late partner and talking with the man's wife.

If she had any doubts about the circumstances surrounding her husband's death...

Callie thought of Mikki and shuddered slightly.

"You okay?" Max asked, when he rejoined her. "You look upset."

"I was just thinking that if Jerry Hawkins does turn out to be the Avenger, it will almost kill his mother. It would devastate Mikki, as well."

"Sure you still want to come along?"

"No, but I've come this far, I may as well see it through."

"Just don't expect too much. Evidence in a case like this usually comes sneaking though the back corners of a dark room and jumps you when you least expect it."

Like a piece of paper with a list on it blowing in the breeze.

Callie felt the now-familiar prickles of fear. Fear for herself, and for Mikki and Abby.

Fear that Jerry Hawkins wasn't the Avenger. And fear that he was.

CHAPTER TWELVE

EVELYN REILLY'S Tudor-style house was tucked away in an upper middle-class neighborhood at the southern end of Sacramento. From the outside, the place looked unassuming, but the inside was tastefully decorated in an eclectic mixture of antiques and contemporary furnishings.

The artwork displayed on the faux painted walls was even more impressive. Most of the paintings were abstracts. Their bold colors and striking graphics seemed to pull you inside them—or push you away. Whichever, the emotional impact was powerful.

"I paint," Evelyn said simply, obviously noting Callie's interest in the artwork as she led them through the wide foyer and into a spacious combination family room and kitchen.

"Did you do all of them?"

"All but the one over the fireplace. That was painted by a friend."

"You have phenomenal talent."

"Thank you. I haven't painted since... I'm not painting now." She turned her attention back to Max. "As I told you when you called, I can't think of any reason why someone from the Courage Bay Police Department would need to see me."

"I'd just like to ask you a few questions. You're not required to answer, and you can kick me out anytime."

She nodded. "Fair enough. Is the kitchen table okay?"

"Kitchen's great," Max said.

"Good. There's more light in here and the view's better."

Callie wasn't sure why that mattered under the circumstances, but the view was nice. A wall of windows overlooked a beautifully landscaped pool.

Evelyn was probably mid-thirties, Callie decided, though she could be older. Her looks were classic, and her smooth blond hair was styled in a sleek bob. She wore stretch, form-fitting capris and a flowing white blouse.

"Can I get you coffee or a soft drink?"

"Nothing for me," Callie said. Now that she was here, she felt uneasy. Max accepted the offer of coffee and made small talk while Evelyn poured it. He asked about a painting over the kitchen table and an antique cookie jar on one of her shelves.

She seemed open enough as she answered his questions, but became edgy when she rejoined them at the table. "Isn't Courage Bay being plagued by a vigilante killer?" she asked, directing her question to Max.

"For the past eight months or so."

"This isn't about that, is it?"

"In a roundabout way," Max explained. "We're looking for patterns in deaths that occurred under unusual circumstances."

Evelyn bristled. "If you're talking about my husband's death, it was an accident, not a murder."

"I know," Max said, "and I realize what an imposition this is. But as part of our investigation, we need to look at every possibility, and that includes freak accidents that happened around the state during the same time period."

"If they're accidents, how can they be connected?"

"Some of the murders appeared to be accidents at first. One victim's house was washed away in a mud slide. Another victim had a roof collapse on him. Another died in a plane crash."

Evelyn hugged her cup as if warming her hands. "I didn't know. Nonetheless, Travis's death was an accident."

"The police report mentioned eyewitnesses who thought differently," Max said.

"They were wrong. The man on the scaffolding with Travis that day was his partner, Jerry Hawkins. There was no way Jerry pushed him. They were tighter than brothers."

"Good to know." Max sipped his coffee.

Callie tried to stay quiet like she'd promised, but she had so many questions she needed answered. "Are you certain there were no problems between the two of them?" she asked. "Arguments about money or the direction the company was going?"

Max glared at Callie. She ignored him and focused on Evelyn, hoping for some indication that her question had struck a nerve. If it had, Evelyn covered it well.

"They argued all the time," Evelyn said, a trace of a smile crossing her face. "Both of them were as hard-headed as two bricks. But when the arguments were over, they'd have a few beers together and forget about it."

"Jerry Hawkins must have been pretty broken up about Travis's death," Max said.

"He was at the hospital every day after the accident. Jerry was a rock for me, even though I know he was hurting almost as bad as I was." She lowered her eyes and her voice. "As I still am."

"I'm sure," Max said quietly. "Losing someone you love must be devastating."

Evelyn bit her bottom lip and blinked rapidly, as if working hard to hold back the tears. Callie hurt for Evelyn, but still she wondered if the woman might have underestimated the arguments between her husband and Jerry. Perhaps it had been guilt that had made Jerry so attentive to his partner and his partner's wife after the accident. Or maybe Jerry was in love with Evelyn.

"You probably know that Jerry Hawkins has family in Courage Bay," Max said, breaking the silence once Evelyn had regained her composure.

Evelyn exhaled sharply. "I should have known there was more to this than you admitted. You must know his mother lives in Courage Bay. You probably also know that his sister, Elizabeth, lives in Los Angeles."

"Makes perfect sense for him to visit them," Max said. "A man needs family."

"More often they need him. He was supportive of his mother during her divorce and his sister during her struggle with drug addiction."

Callie had never heard about Elizabeth's problems. Now she understood why Abby volunteered in the addiction unit of the hospital. His sister's experience might also explain Jerry's contempt for Bernie Brusco. Callie's suspicions about Jerry could be a case of serious misjudgment.

But she wasn't totally convinced. Not yet, anyway. None of what she'd learned explained why he was spending so much time in Courage Bay now, attending social gatherings, when he'd never done so in the past. Nor did it explain the injury that supposedly kept him from working.

"Was Jerry hurt trying to save your husband?" Callie asked.

"No. He tried to grab Travis and missed. That was it."

"So when do you expect him back in Sacramento?" Max asked.

"That's up to him."

"And the way his injury heals, I guess," Callie said, determined to find out the truth.

Evelyn shrugged. "I have no clue what you're talking about. Jerry's not injured. He needed time away from the company. There's no law against that."

"None that I know of," Max agreed.

Evelyn's elbow caught the edge of the napkin and sent it flying to the floor. She reached to pick it up, and when she looked at them again, it was as if she'd come to a decision.

"I'd like you to leave now," she said. "You're wasting your time and mine. Jerry Hawkins is hard-nosed, determined and sometimes arrogant. But he has a heart of gold, and he's not your killer. I'd stake my life on that."

For Mikki's sake, Callie hoped Evelyn was right.

IT WAS AFTER SIX that evening when the plane touched down on the runway and the passengers started gathering their baggage from the overhead compartments. Max took out his cell phone and turned it on to retrieve his messages.

The first two messages dealt with routine situations. The third was a report that a body had been found not more than ten minutes ago, probably while the plane was taxiing down the tarmac.

White female, approximately thirty years of age, long blond hair, found stuffed in a Dumpster at Courage Bay Hospital. The victim was naked, with a stethoscope dangling from her severely bruised neck.

CALLIE'S ANXIETY SOARED as she listened to Max's end of his phone conversation. There was a new murder victim, and somehow the case was related to the hospital.

"Who is it?" she asked, the second he broke the connection.

"Unidentified female. I have to go to the crime scene, but I'll drop you off at police headquarters on the way. I'll arrange for an officer to take you home."

She didn't wait for him to finish the conversation before she grabbed her own cell phone and punched in Mikki's cell number. The ringing seemed interminable. Finally she heard the damn recorded voice saying to leave a message at the tone.

There was no reason to panic. Mikki was probably making hospital rounds or with a patient. Or… Callie tried the number to Mikki's office. Gone for the day, as she expected. "Exactly where did they find the body?"

"Stuffed in a Dumpster back of the hospital."

"How old was the victim?"

He wrapped his arm around her, but didn't slow his walk. "Don't jump to conclusions. There's no evidence at this point that the death is associated with the Avenger. It could be domestic violence. Probably not anyone you know."

Mikki. He was thinking Mikki, too, but he wouldn't say it. She couldn't, either. But the dread was so thick inside her she could barely breathe. "What age?"

He guided her into the elevator to the parking garage. "Somewhere around thirty."

"Blond?"

"Yeah." He pulled her into his arms and held on tightly as the elevator began its ascent. "I know what you've been through, but you have to hang tough, Callie. Don't go imagining the worst when all we know is that a young woman's body was discovered."

But she couldn't hang tough, not anymore. She'd known instinctively that Mikki was in danger, and all she'd done was fly off to Sacramento to hear another of Jerry Hawkins's admirers describe how great he was.

If they were wrong… If Callie's suspicions had been right… If Mikki was… The elevator bell clanged and the door slid open.

"I'm going with you, Max."

"That's not an option."

"No. It's a fact. With you or without you. I'm going to the hospital."

He opened his mouth to argue, then clamped it shut and took her arm as they made their way through the packed parking garage.

"You can go to the hospital with me," he said, "but the crime scene is off-limits. And that's nonnegotiable."

She'd expected as much. But she just had to know the identity of the victim. She tried Mikki's number again on the way to the hospital, praying she would hear Mikki's cheery voice say hello.

The prayer and the phone went unanswered.

THE SCENE AT THE HOSPITAL bordered on bedlam despite the presence of a dozen police officers, some working inside the area bound by yellow police tape, others keeping back the media camera crews and the curious.

Callie climbed from the police car. She was still having trouble breathing, but the familiar setting of the hospital gave her a sense of control. She headed toward the nearest entry, a back door used for deliveries.

Once inside the hospital, she was surrounded by a group of nurses, all of them red-eyed. One woman Callie knew only by sight was sobbing openly.

"He killed her. The rotten bastard finally killed her."

Callie put her hand to the wall for support. "Who?"

"Her husband. He wouldn't let her go. They were legally separated, but the sick, demented bastard wouldn't let her go."

Husband. Callie sucked in a breath of ammonia-scented air. "Is there a positive identification of the victim?"

"The victim is Sally Raye McManus, a third floor R.N. who works the second shift."

Callie spun around at the sound of Max's voice. He was standing in the doorway she'd just entered, his broad shoulders blocking most of the glare from the setting sun. Relief flooded her senses, quickly followed by guilt. Sally Raye McManus had obviously been a friend of these nurses, even as Mikki was her friend. Sally was also someone's daughter, maybe a sister. Maybe a mom.

"Thanks, Max. Thanks for the information." She started to go to him, then felt the constraints of watching eyes and settled for letting their gazes meet.

"Your assistant is on the way," Max said. "He wants you to stay right where you are until he arrives."

It took Callie a second to understand that he was

talking about Ted Gravier, the cop assigned to protect her. She nodded and swallowed hard. The nurses believed that Sally's husband had killed her, but it could have been the Avenger. Maybe Sally had taken Callie's spot as number eight.

Was Callie now number nine or ten or eleven? Who knew how many more people would die before the man who meted out justice met his own.

Max sat in the easy chair that provided a view to the back of Callie's property and the rolling ocean beyond. Pickering had deserted his mistress and fallen asleep at Max's feet. Every so often he moved his head back and forth and tapped the floor with his tail, probably dreaming he was chasing birds along the beach and wondering why he was being walked by a neighbor's son these days instead of Callie.

Max slipped his Smith & Wesson from his shoulder holster and ran his thumb along the grip. Another murder in Courage Bay. This one was not related to the Avenger. The victim's estranged husband had already confessed to the crime.

The number of murders was climbing in a city that had previously had the lowest murder rate per capita in southern California. Courage Bay. Max's town. The one he had sworn to protect.

Today's killer was behind bars, but the Avenger was still on the loose, and Max was no closer to arresting him than he had been a month ago. The only real evidence pointed toward Henry Lalane. Henry was being tailed twenty-four hours a day, and Max had men investigating every corner of his past, determining if Henry had ever learned to handle a gun with the accuracy the Avenger had demonstrated.

Max pointed his own gun toward the window, holding it steady, as if he were aiming to fire. Pickering roused and nudged his nose a little closer before going back to sleep.

Max laid the loaded pistol on the table beside him, toed off his shoes and leaned back, letting his head relax against the pillow. He was already drifting off to sleep when he heard Pickering growl. A low sound deep in his throat.

Jerking awake, Max reached for his weapon. Pickering was on his haunches now, looking toward the window.

"What is it, boy? Did you hear something?"

Pickering barked and ran toward the back door. Max's veins burned from the rush of adrenaline as he followed the dog. The moon was bright and Max could see most of the back deck. There was no sign of movement there or beyond. Even Pickering settled down again.

A false alarm. Still, Max wouldn't rest until he was sure. He opened the back door slowly and stepped outside. And that's when he heard it.

Tick. Tick. Tick. Like a clock.

Or a bomb.

CHAPTER THIRTEEN

PANIC ROARED in Max's head, drowning out everything but the low, menacing threat of the ticking bomb. Options flew at him from all sides, darting around in his mind like ricocheting bullets. He had to get Callie away from the house before the bomb exploded.

He yelled for her as he rushed back inside. He took the steps three at a time, adrenaline pumping so fast and furiously he didn't feel the exertion. He caught her just as she reached the landing. She was barefoot, still poking her arms through a blue silk robe that trailed behind her.

She practically fell into his arms. "What's wrong?"

"We have to get out of here," he ordered. "Fast." He took hold of her hand and raced with her down the rest of the stairs.

"What's happened? Why is Pickering barking like that?"

"I think there's a bomb planted somewhere on your deck." His voice cracked like his nerves as he dragged her toward the door. "Don't ask questions, Callie. Just run."

"I can't leave Pickering..." Callie broke from Max's grasp and dashed toward the back door. Max tried to catch her, but she was too fast. By the time he reached her, she was already pushing onto the deck and screaming for Pickering.

Max spotted the retriever rooting around a large bush at the edge of the pool. The ticking seemed deafening to Max, and sweat streamed down his brow and into his eyes. He yelled at Pickering to follow them as he swooped Callie up in his arms and began to run with her, away from the house and toward the pounding surf.

"Ohmigod!" Callie screamed and went rigid in Max's arms.

He glanced behind them. Pickering was a few feet away, a wood and metal contraption dangling from his mouth. Pickering was following, but he was bringing the bomb with him.

There was no way to outrun the retriever. No way to outrun the bomb.

"Run to the water, Callie. Please, just run and don't look back." He set her feet on the sand and tried to catch Pickering as he raced by. But it was all a game to the retriever. He dodged Max and began to run in circles, still holding tightly to the bomb.

And then Max heard Callie's voice, too close, shaky, but probably as calm as she could make it. "Hand it to me, Pickering. Good dog. Hand me the toy, and we'll play catch."

Pickering stopped running, studied Max for what seemed like an eternity, then shuffled over and dropped the bomb at Callie's feet. Max swooped down, picked it up and hurled it down the beach as far away from them as he could. There was no way to know if it was far enough.

He grabbed Callie's arm and started running. This time she kept up with him, and so did Pickering, yelping as if Max had stolen a prize possession.

They didn't stop until they reached the rolling waves of the ocean. Callie's feet tangled with Pickering, and she fell to the sand, dragging Max down with her.

The cold waves washed over them, splashing into their faces and drenching their clothes. They rolled away from the water, holding on to each other as an explosion rocked the ground and sent a dark pillar of smoke into the air.

Max couldn't speak, wouldn't have known what to say if he could. All he knew was that he'd died a thousand deaths when he thought he might have failed Callie.

So he just held her while his insides slowly shook back into place.

IT WAS AFTER 2:00 A.M., hours after the bomb had exploded on the beach without delivering major damage, but Callie was still wide-awake, her nerves shot to hell and back, her system revved from the pot of coffee she'd downed since arriving at Max's apartment.

"Be good if you can get some sleep," said the young cop assigned to protect her. "I've got everything under control."

"I'm too wired." She walked over to the counter where the officer was smearing some peanut butter on a slice of white bread. All she could remember of his name was Bo. "Do you think Max will be much longer?" she asked.

"Hard to say." He slapped on another slice of bread and tore off a paper towel to use as a napkin. "He'll probably stay right there with the crime-scene unit. And they won't leave until they've gathered every smidgen of evidence. The bomb team's probably still there, too. It's just one big party."

"A party?"

"Just an expression," he assured her. "They're plenty serious. They are with every case, but they've got the chief breathing down their necks tonight. That'll really keep them on their toes."

Callie stepped over Pickering, who was stretched out in the middle of Max's tiny kitchen, fast asleep.

"I may lie down awhile," Callie said, "but if I fall asleep tell Max to wake me when he gets here."

The cop swallowed and dabbed at his mouth with the paper towel. "I'll give him the message. And don't you worry. I may sound a little country, but I know what I'm doing." His gaze went to the pistol on the table. "I'm the best shot on the force two years running."

She nodded, sure he was as good as he claimed. Max had specifically requested him and had pulled the officer from his regular assignment to come stand guard until Max returned.

She went back to Max's bedroom, still not ready for sleep but thinking she'd at least lie down. She'd missed work yesterday, and tired or not, she had to see patients and keep her administrative appointments today.

The apartment was like Max, she thought. Sparsely furnished with nothing but the necessities. Clean, functional and understated.

The bedroom even smelled of Max. A faint scent of aftershave, musky, like walking in the woods on a summer day. All man. That was Max. Unreadable at times, yet tonight, when he'd held her as they'd breathed in the ocean air in pure relief, she'd felt closer to him than she'd ever felt to any man.

It had been far more intimate than the sizzle Mikki talked about. More intense than the hot need that Callie felt stirring her blood whenever Max touched or kissed her. And totally different from anything she'd felt with his cousin Tony.

But this was not the time to be thinking of any of this. Or maybe it was, she decided, walking to the bed and collapsing on top of the crisp white sheets. She and Max had come within seconds of losing their lives tonight. The killer who had targeted her had almost destroyed both of them. Life was precious, and it came with no guarantees.

Life could be lost in a split second, the way it had probably been for Mary. One minute she'd been full of life. The next she'd been dead.

Callie trembled as tears stung the back of her eyelids. She did need some rest. The emotional roller coaster of the past week and tonight's brush with death were wearing her down. She scanned the room for a box of tissues. When she didn't see any, she slid open the top drawer of Max's bedside table.

Her own image stared back at her. Stunned, she picked up the photograph and studied it closely. She couldn't remember when it had been taken, but it was years ago, when she'd been married to Tony.

Reaching back into the drawer, she picked up three more photographs, all of her. Her mind whirled for a second, the fatigue and caffeine combining to confound her. Old photographs of her in the drawer by Max's bed. Why?

Unless... Unless, as Mikki would say, he had a real thing for her—and it had been going on for a long, long time.

If so, he'd never acted on his feelings, never given him and Callie a chance to see if things might work out between them. She wanted that chance—and she didn't want to wait until this nightmare with the Avenger was over. She wanted to be with Max tonight. Tomorrow was a gamble at best. The present was all they could be sure of.

She wanted to make love with Max now, and this time she wouldn't take no for an answer.

"WHAT DO YOU MEAN you don't know where he is?" Max demanded. "We had a 24/7 on Lalane."

"He left his house at 11:08. We followed him down to San Moritz Avenue, then lost him when he cut into a line of traffic on the freeway approach. We tried to pick him up again, but he just seemed to disappear."

"So where is he now?"

"Boating, it seems. We located his car at a marina on Ocean Drive. We're just sitting here in the marina parking lot waiting on him to get back."

Max muttered a couple of choice curses under his breath. Henry Lalane didn't have a boat of his own. Max had checked that out long ago when they'd first started running profiles on dozens of potential suspects. But the attorney could have rented one or borrowed one. Over half the population of Courage Bay owned some kind of watercraft.

With the right kind of boat, the guy could have docked near Callie's house but down the beach and out of sight. From there it would have been fairly easy to sneak onto her deck, plant the bomb and then disappear behind a neighbor's house until the path was clear for him to escape.

He'd have had to work out all the details in advance, but when hadn't the Avenger done that?

The Courage Bay district attorney as the Avenger? As far as Max was concerned, the possibility became more likely with every passing second. And even if tonight's crime scene didn't net them any new evidence, the fingerprints on the note with Callie's name on it and Lalane's untimely disappearance were sufficient to bring the D.A. in for a formal interrogation.

That is if he reappeared. Frustrated, Max walked back to the crime van, which the team was loading up.

He talked with the officers for a minute, then crawled behind the wheel of his own car. The second he did, Callie slipped back into his mind, not that she'd ever been totally out of it.

Max had walked into dangerous situations more times than he cared to count, and the most he'd felt was a rush of adrenaline and sometimes a quickening of his pulse. But he'd come close to losing Callie to a deranged killer tonight, and his whole being had become one giant ball of panic and fear.

He had to keep her safe. He couldn't think beyond that right now. Couldn't think about wanting her. Couldn't think about tasting her lips. Couldn't let himself start fantasizing about what it would be like to make love with her.

He was closing in on the Avenger, and he had to keep his mind and priorities crystal clear. Making love with Callie was out of the question.

CALLIE WAS LYING in Max's bed in the dark but still wide-awake when Max returned. She heard his voice mingling with Bo's, then the sound of the door opening and the click of the dead lock sliding into place when Bo left. Seconds later she heard a squeak and saw a rectangle of light sneak in around the partially opened bedroom door.

"I'm awake," she murmured.

"It's almost 3:00 a.m."

"I drank lots of coffee. How did the investigation go?"

"We'll know more when we get reports back from forensics and the bomb team, but it looks as if the bomb was a serious weapon, enough that if it had exploded on your deck, it would have likely taken out most of the house and sent the rest into a ball of flames."

"The Avenger?"

"That would be my guess."

"I'd like to hear all about it in the morning."

"Good. You need to try to get some sleep. I need to shower."

She hadn't planned it that way, but now that Callie thought about it, the shower idea sounded perfect. "Do that," she said. She waited until she heard the sound of running water, then slipped her legs over the side of the bed and tiptoed into the bathroom.

Max's naked body was a mere silhouette behind the curtain, yet she trembled and held her breath.

"Is something wrong?" he asked, his hands clutching the soap and washcloth against his chest.

"Too many things," she whispered. She opened her arms and let the cotton robe she'd brought with her slip from her shoulders. "That's why I need something in my life that's totally right. I need you."

She heard the catch in his breath and knew he wasn't prepared for this. But she wouldn't be daunted. Not by speeches of more appropriate timing and duty. And not by some unwritten cop rules that made no sense to her. Not when Max had photographs of her next to his bed.

Not when she wanted him so badly that her body seemed to be melting at the core.

She pushed back the shower curtain and joined him. For a second he just stared at her, his gaze roaming her body, a look of stunned amazement on his face.

"Callie."

Her name sounded more like a cry when it crossed his lips. She stepped under the spray and placed her hands on his soapy chest. "Let me do that for you," she whispered, taking the soap and cloth from his hands.

"You shouldn't... We shouldn't..." His words dissolved in a low moan as she took the cloth and ran it over his abdomen, dipping so low that her hand brushed his erection.

"We should," she whispered. "We're lucky to be alive. And I want you so very, very much."

And then she was in his arms, his lips on hers, their bodies slick and soapy as they slid against each other, the warm water cascading over them. The hesitancy Max had exhibited before dissipated in a whirl of steam and heat and passion.

He devoured her, starting with her lips, but moving down her neck to her pebbled nipples. He cradled her breasts in his hands as he sucked and nibbled, then took her in his arms again and lifted her so that her intimate places pressed against his arousal.

"Oh, Callie, tell me this is real and that you're not going to disappear the way you always do in my dreams."

"I'm not going anywhere, Max Zirinsky."

Only she was. She was flying right toward paradise. Her body tingled on the outside and ran hot and golden on the inside. He ran one hand between her legs, and her own moisture mingled with the water from the shower.

"Oh, Callie, I've dreamed of this so long."

He lifted her again, and this time she wrapped her legs around him. He slid inside her, and she gasped in pleasure, then tried in vain to bite back squeals of ecstasy as he thrust deeper and deeper.

His breathing quickened and his body grew taut, finally erupting inside her, taking her with him. It was long seconds later before she loosened her legs from around him and he let her feet slide back down to the tub.

There were questions in her mind, but she didn't want to ask them now. She didn't want to talk at all, because there was no way to avoid speaking about the Avenger. And she wouldn't let this moment be spoiled with talk of death and danger and the demented mind of a man who'd made himself a vindictive God.

Finally Max broke the soft, sweet silence. "First thing I've ever known that was worth an eight-year wait," he whispered as he reached behind him and turned off the water.

She stepped out of the tub and reached for a towel. "Let's not wait that long to do it again."

"No. I was thinking eight minutes tops."

She'd have been up for that, but eight minutes later, Max was fast asleep. Callie cuddled close. Nothing about her life had changed. She was likely still the next victim on the Avenger's list. She still feared for Mikki and grieved for Mary, but her heart felt totally different as she let the rhythmic sounds of Max's breathing lull her to sleep.

MAX WOKE AT THE FIRST gray light of dawn, immediately conscious of the sweet truth that he'd made love with Callie and that she was lying beside him in his bed. He'd never be able to count the nights he'd lain in this same bed, thoughts of her keeping him awake.

He'd imagined her as his wife. Even conjured up images of the life they might have had if things had been different. A houseful of kids. Well, maybe not a houseful, but a couple anyway. A boy that he'd teach to fish and play baseball. A girl that he'd—actually, he'd never figured out what he'd do with a little girl except give her hugs and hold her on his shoulders to watch the Fourth of July and the Christmas parades go by.

Stupid dreams that never had a chance of coming true, since he and Callie came from different worlds.

Not that she was a snob in any sense of the word. But when the newness of the relationship wore off and the passion cooled, the differences between them would become all too obvious.

But tonight none of that seemed to matter. Callie was here and she was safe and alive. He could hear her breathing and feel the warmth of her body. He snuggled closer and let his right hand creep across her to cup her breast. Desire hit again with such force he felt as though his heart might jump right out of his chest.

He let the flat of his hand slide down her abdomen until his fingers tangled in the curly hairs at the apex of her thighs. She squirmed in her sleep and gave a slight moan. He shouldn't wake her, but there was no way he could go back to sleep without—

The piercing ring of a phone jarred every nerve in his body and woke Callie.

"It can't be morning," she muttered. "Throw that idiot alarm clock out the window."

"I think that's your cell phone. Any idea where it is?"

She groaned. "Too close." But she untangled herself from the sheets and padded across the floor to retrieve it from her purse.

He listened to her conversation long enough to know it had to do with a patient, not a killer, then wiggled into a pair of jeans and headed for the bathroom to relieve himself and gargle with mouthwash. He glanced at the clock on the way: 5:00 a.m.

Callie was hanging up the phone when he returned to the bedroom. "An emergency?" he asked.

"Afraid so. One of the residents at the Keller Center was just rushed to the hospital with complications and early labor."

"What hospital?"

"Courage Bay. They don't usually use our hospital, but this time they made an exception."

"Why is that?"

"The patient's an emotionally fragile fifteen-year-old expecting twins, and she insisted that they take her to my hospital, though she knows I don't deliver babies." Callie walked over to him and slipped her arms around his neck. "I could use a good morning kiss."

The kiss blew him away and he had to concentrate hard to get his mind back to where it should be if they weren't going to make love again this morning. He watched as she paraded to his closet and pulled out the clean slacks and cotton sweater she'd brought with her last night.

It wasn't so much that she was flaunting her nudity as that she was comfortable with it. Max wasn't even sure she knew that he was so aroused he could barely function.

"Fill me in on details while I dress," she said. "What kind of information did you pick up last night?"

"I'm going to bring Henry Lalane in for questioning today," he said, cutting to the chase.

"Really? I thought you had a tail on him," she said, pulling on a pair of white, lacy panties.

Max swallowed hard and turned away before he lost control and tore the panties off. "I did, but they lost him for almost four hours. Didn't find him until I was getting out of the car here last night."

"Oh, no! This looks bad for him, doesn't it?"

Max nodded. "It's starting to."

"I don't buy that a man like Henry Lalane can be the Avenger. People don't just suddenly change from a law-abiding citizen to a criminal."

"Happens all the time," Max said. "You think Henry can't be the Avenger, but you think Jerry Hawkins could be. Is that just because you haven't known him all your life the way you have Henry?"

"Of course not." She reached behind her to fasten her bra, then leaned over to adjust her breasts in the cups. "He just seems more guilty."

"Evelyn Reilly wouldn't agree with you."

Max pulled a shirt from its hanger and poked his arms through the sleeves. If Callie was in a hurry to get to the hospital, he'd best be in a hurry, too. He had to drive her there and stay with her until she was safely in the hands of her intern cop.

Max quickly finished dressing. Last night seemed more like a dream than ever as the cold reality of another day set in. But a dream was better than a nightmare seven nights a week.

"PUSH, GAIL. Breathe and push. Breathe and push."

"I'm trying." Gail squeezed Callie's hand so hard that Callie winced in pain. Gail's water had broken during the night, but she hadn't mentioned the fact to the nurse on duty at the center until quarter to five in the morning. By then the first labor pains had started, and Gail had already dilated three centimeters.

"It hurts," Gail whimpered, then screamed as the next contraction hit.

"I know. You can have lots of pain reliever when this is over. Right now we just want to get the babies out safely."

"They'll be too little. They'll *dieeee!*" The last word came out another high-pitched wail.

"Lots of premature babies are healthy," Callie assured her, praying these two were.

"First head's coming out," Dr. Jergens announced.

Callie leaned closer to Gail. "Here it comes, sweetie. Push for all you're worth."

Gail pushed and screamed and the head popped out, followed by a bloody, squirming body. "It's a girl," the doctor announced. "Got the winner. Let's go for place."

Callie stole a look at the newborn as the doctor cut the umbilical cord and handed her off to the nurse. She was small, but she was breathing and her lungs seemed to be working fine.

The process started again. This time the contractions seemed to be harder, or else Gail was so tired from the ordeal that her pain tolerance had diminished.

Gail started crying. "I want my mother. Did somebody call my mother?"

"You're the mother now" was on the tip of Callie's tongue, but she bit back the words. It wasn't the time for lectures. The second baby's head was pushing through.

Sweat beaded on the doctor's forehead as the rest of the newborn's body slid into the world. "This one's a corker. Gonna give his sister a hard time."

"It's a boy," Callie cried. "You did it, Gail. They're both out and kicking."

"They're all right? You're sure?"

"As far as I can tell right now. Dr. Mikki will check them out once they're cleaned up and in the incubator. Do you want to see them?"

"Sure."

The nurse handed the girl to Gail, then without asking, she put the boy in Callie's arms. He punched his tiny fists out from beneath the light blanket and opened his mouth like a baby bird waiting for breakfast.

He was so adorable. Callie rocked him gently, holding him close to her heart.

"You could take them, Dr. Baker. Please. They need you."

Callie's heart constricted. "You don't know what you're asking, Gail."

"I do. You already love him. I can tell."

"He's precious. Any woman who adopts him will love him. She'll love them both."

"Not like you would. Please. Take them home with you. Be their mom."

Callie's body grew warm, and a giant lump balled in her throat. She handed the baby back to the nurse. She had to get out of the delivery room, had to breathe fresh air and get control of her senses before Gail had her considering the ridiculous request.

"Will you at least think about it?" Gail begged, her lips quivering as if she were about to start crying again.

"I'll think about it."

It was the wrong answer. Callie couldn't imagine

where it had come from or why she was shaking when she walked out of the delivery room. All she knew was that her heart ached and her arms felt so incredibly empty.

CHAPTER FOURTEEN

CALLIE'S RECEPTIONIST met her as she exited an examining room. "You have a call on line one from Mrs. Marjorie Craven. She says it's an emergency. Do you want to take it or call her back?"

"I'll take it." Callie motioned to Ted that he didn't have to follow her into her office. She had him set up at a desk just inside the reception area so that he could see down the hallway and hear her if she called to him rather than have him in and out of examining rooms, breaching her patients' privacy.

Both Marjorie and the judge were Callie's patients. Marjorie had been in for her annual exam just a few weeks ago, but it had been quite awhile since the judge had come in to see Callie.

"Hello, Marjorie, what seems to be the problem?"

"It's Lawrence."

"Is he sick?"

"I don't know. He flew to San Francisco yesterday, and when he came in last night, he didn't look well. This morning he said he didn't feel like going to work."

"Is he feverish or experiencing nausea?"

"No. But he's sick, really sick. I found him outside a few minutes ago, standing by the cliff, staring into space and muttering incoherently. At first he didn't even seem to recognize me. Then all of a sudden, he snapped out of it. I think he may have had a seizure."

"Is he still incoherent?"

"No, but he's irrational. He refused to let me drive him to your office or the hospital emergency room. When I tried to talk to him about it, he stormed out of the house. He's out there now in the heat. I know you're busy, but is there any way you could get away and come here to see him?"

"It would be a lot better if he came to the hospital."

"I know, but he won't, and he has to see a doctor."

There was no mistaking the panic in Marjorie's voice. Callie understood her fears. This was totally unlike Judge Craven and it did indeed sound as if he'd had a seizure or perhaps a mild stroke. "I'll be there as quickly as I can, Marjorie. In the meantime, try to get him to come in and lie down. If he collapses or becomes incoherent again, you should call for an ambulance at once."

"I will."

Callie made a few notes on the chart of the patient she'd just seen, but Judge Craven was front and center in her mind. He'd looked fine when she and Max had run into him at the airport yesterday. She hoped this was nothing serious, but the symptoms Marjorie described were reason for concern.

Callie saw her last two morning appointments, then washed her hands and grabbed her medical bag. "Ready for a road trip, Ted?"

He smiled. "Am I ever?"

"What's the matter? Don't you like doctors' offices?"

"One notch above standing in line at the unemployment office or digging ditches. So where are we going?"

"We're making a house call."

"Anyone I know?"

"Judge Lawrence Craven."

"Whoa!" He grabbed her arm and pulled her to a stop before she reached the door leading into the hospital corridor. "Have you checked this out with the chief?"

"I don't have to ask Max if I can do my job. Besides, I have you for protection. You do have bullets in your gun, don't you?"

"I've got plenty of bullets. That's not the issue. The chief said to make certain you don't go into any situations where protection could be compromised."

"How can protection be compromised if I'm only visiting the house of a sick patient?"

"The Cravens don't have a house. They have an estate. I worked a party detail there a few years back. A small army could camp on the grounds."

"No small armies out there today. Marjorie wouldn't let them walk on her grass."

"All the same, I have to check this out with the chief first."

"Fine. Check all you want, once we're on the road. My car or yours?"

"Mine. Definitely mine, in case the chief says to turn around and bring you right back to the hospital."

They were almost at Ted's car when she heard a male voice shout her name from across the parking lot. She turned toward the voice, and caught a glimpse of Ted's hand moving to the butt of his gun before she saw Jerry Hawkins stepping out from between two parked SUVs.

"Could I help you with something?" she said, irritated that he'd tracked her down this way.

"Yeah. You can tell me why the hell you went all the way to Sacramento to harass Evelyn Reilly?"

"I beg your pardon."

"Don't act like you don't know what I'm talking about. Evelyn described you to a T."

"I think you need to move on and not bother the doctor," Ted said.

Callie was all too aware that Ted was ready to pull out the gun at a moment's notice. "It's okay, Ted. Let him talk."

Jerry leaned against the door of Ted's car. "No, you're the one who should talk, Callie. What's your problem with me? Is it because I like your friend Mikki and she likes me? Because if it is, get over it. I'm crazy about her, and unless she sends me packing, I'm not going away."

"Mikki's my friend. I don't want her hurt."

"And what makes you think I'd hurt her? Because I

don't like drug dealers? Well, go spend some time in the streets instead of in your cozy little beach house, Callie Baker. See what dealers do to people's lives. Then see if you give a damn when one is eliminated."

"Murder is never justified."

"Yeah, well, that's you. I'm me. Stay away from Evelyn. She's been through enough."

He stormed away without giving her a chance to respond. Not that she had a decent response. If the evidence wasn't so strong against Henry Lalane, Jerry's outburst today would have only added to her suspicion that he had something to hide.

But the way things looked now, when this was over, she might owe Jerry Hawkins an apology.

MARJORIE OPENED the front door before Callie had time to ring the doorbell. She stared at Ted. "Who is he?"

"This is Ted Gravier," Callie said. "He's an intern who's working with me." She glanced around. "Where's our patient?"

"I need to talk to you before you see him. But just you, not *him*." Marjorie glared at Ted as if he were an alien who'd shown up uninvited for dinner.

"No problem," Callie agreed, though she knew Ted wouldn't like it. Max had been in the interrogation room with Henry when Ted had called, and he'd been forced to leave the message about their destination with someone else. Ted had seemed uneasy about not speaking with Max. Either the young officer was extremely cautious or he wasn't convinced Lalane was the man who'd added Callie's name to the victim list and planted a bomb beneath her kitchen window.

But as far as Callie was concerned, the Cravens were not a concern. Marjorie was a dear, and the judge was a California gentleman through and through.

"We can talk in the study," Marjorie said, leading the way. She turned back to Ted. "You can wait in here. If my husband returns, I'd appreciate it if you'd let me know at once."

"Yes, ma'am."

Marjorie closed the door behind them, creating a conspiratorial atmosphere. "I didn't fully level with you on the phone, Callie. This isn't the first time Lawrence has had one of these blackout spells that leave him momentarily confused and incoherent. It's just this one was worse than the others."

"Worse in what way?"

"He usually snaps back immediately and seems perfectly normal. But he's still acting strangely."

Blackouts. Periods of confusion. Incoherency. Things were beginning to add up. "How long has he exhibited these symptoms?"

"About six months?"

"Has he sought any medical help with this?"

"No. He refuses to see anyone. Abby Hawkins says he's in denial. Abby's the only one who knows about this," Marjorie added, as if she owed Callie an explanation. "She's been through so much with her daughter that she understands how hard it is to stand by and watch someone you love refuse to seek help. She offered to come over today since I was so upset, but I told her you were coming."

"I can't do a lot here, Marjorie. Lawrence needs diagnostic tests and those can only be conducted in the hospital." And if her instincts were right, the diagnosis would not be good.

"I think he's afraid of what you'll find. He's never been sick, you know. He's so careful to eat right and exercise."

"Unfortunately, that's not always enough." Callie had a full schedule of appointments this afternoon and she wanted to get back to see Gail and the babies. But right now Judge Craven was her top priority. "Where is Lawrence now?"

"He's outside in the gardens. I'm not sure exactly where."

When Callie and Marjorie returned to the living area, they found Ted standing by the window, scanning the grounds.

"Have you seen Judge Craven?" Callie asked.

"Is he wearing dark blue slacks and a light blue checked sport shirt?" Ted asked.

"Yes," Marjorie answered.

"Then I saw him a few minutes ago, just beyond the fountain."

"We should be able to find him easily enough," Callie said. "Why don't you wait here, Marjorie? He may be more receptive to my arguments for getting the proper care if you're not around."

"If you think that's best."

"I do." She would have preferred Ted stay as well, but she knew there wasn't a chance he'd let her venture out on the grounds without him.

"So what's supposed to be wrong with this guy?" Ted asked, once they were outside. "He didn't look sick when I saw him."

"I'm not sure. Max and I ran into him at the airport yesterday and he mentioned having a friend who had an inoperable brain tumor. Now I'm thinking he might be the one who has the tumor. The symptoms fit. And people frequently say a friend has a problem when they're actually the one."

"Why would he do that?"

"He might think he's protecting Marjorie by not telling her the truth, especially if he's seen a doctor and the tumor or tumors are inoperable."

"One of those guys who likes to tough it out alone, huh?"

"It's plausible." She pushed up her sleeve and glanced at her watch. "Tell you what, I'm running low on time, so let's split up. You take the right side of the garden, I'll take the left. First one who spots the judge calls for the other."

"My job is to stay with you at all times."

"You're not making this easy."

"Easy wasn't one of the chief's orders."

Ted stuck to her like glue as they strolled the path by the rose garden and then turned onto a more narrow one that led back to the view of the Pacific from the cliff. That was the farthest point from the house, but from there they could work their way back down the other side of the garden. If they didn't find him by then, Callie would have to go back to the hospital without him.

They were almost at the cliff when she heard the crack of gunfire. A second later, she saw the blood running down the back of Ted's neck, the crimson stain spreading across his shirt. He staggered a few steps and collapsed onto the plush lawn.

Callie fell to the ground beside him and grabbed his wrist, praying for a pulse. There was none. Still, she dragged Ted's lifeless body behind a low hedge that separated two sections of the English garden.

Her mind spun while she tried in vain to revive him. Someone else was here with them. Someone besides Judge Craven. If it was the Avenger, then the bullet that hit Ted had likely been meant for her.

MAX WAS GETTING NOWHERE with his questioning of Henry Lalane. The guy openly resented that he'd been brought in for questioning and he knew all the angles. Of course, it was also possible Henry was telling the truth and someone was framing him—a possibility that Max couldn't ignore.

"Did you ever go hunting?" Max asked, changing his tactics.

"Be a little difficult since I've already told you I've never fired a gun."

"There's bow hunting."

"Then, no. I've never hunted. I don't kill for fun or recreation, and I buy my meat at the market."

"To each his own." Max leaned back in his chair as if they were a couple of old friends chatting. "You're a smart prosecutor. So what's your story for how your fingerprints got on that square of paper?"

"It's not as if my fingerprints are a rare commodity. I handle legal documents all the time and they end up in all kinds of places. Pretty much anyone who walks into my office could pick up a sheet of paper from my outbox that would likely have my fingerprints on it. And it wouldn't have to be a clean sheet of paper," Lalane added, "since the list was no bigger than half a page."

Max had already thought of that. "Who comes in and out of your office on a regular basis?"

"Secretaries. All the prosecutors and junior prosecutors who work in the office. Friends. Cops from time to time. Judges. Defense attorneys. You name it."

"Judge Craven come by often?"

"I wouldn't say often. He stops in from time to time."

"When was the last time?"

"You're not trying to pin this on Craven, are you? The guy's got enough problems without you hitting him with this."

"What kind of problems does Craven have?"

"He works too hard."

"You and Lawrence Craven go back a long way, don't you? Weren't you and his older brother good friends?"

"So you've done your homework. That doesn't surprise me, Max. I know you're good at what you do, but you're wasting your time trying to pin the avenger murders on me or Lawrence."

"Could be. I'd like to hear about your friendship with Lawrence's brother all the same."

"There's not much to tell. We were high school friends and later college roommates. My younger brother and Lawrence played football together in high school except for the year Lawrence's father was the ambassador to Saudi Arabia. Lawrence spent that year in a military school."

Now that was news to Max. A guy in military school could very well learn to shoot and might also learn about high-powered rifles and small arms. "Lawrence's sophomore year, wasn't it?" Max asked, faking it.

"Junior year. You had to be a junior to get in Summarall."

Max scribbled a note, then went to the door and motioned for one of the officers manning a desk to come get it. "Let me know the second you get something," he said. "I want it on the double."

"Tell me again about the day Lorna Sinke was shot."

Max listened carefully, hoping for some inconsistency in the story Henry had told him right after the hostage situation. There was none. If the man was a liar, he was incredibly good at it. Max was fast losing faith that he was questioning the right man. Still, he wasn't quite ready to release Henry.

"You said you were just hanging out on Leo Garapedian's boat by yourself last night."

"That's what I said. I've got a key and a standing invitation to use it. There's no law against that."

"Just seems odd, going out like that in the middle of the night by yourself."

Henry spread his hands on the table. "Okay, Max. I didn't want to talk about this, but you're not going to let it go until I do. Today would have been my daughter's sixteenth birthday if she hadn't been killed. I couldn't handle being in the house with all the old memories last night, so I went down to the marina and spent some time in the Garapedians' boat. You lose a daughter, you have nights like that. Lots of them."

The story got to Max. Lalane could be playing the old emotional game. There was no way to really know. But losing a daughter could make a man do strange things.

And if Henry wasn't guilty, Max was back to square one.

As soon as Callie realized there was nothing she could do for Ted, her own survival instincts checked in. She took off running, darting among the bushes for cover. She had no clue who she was running from or if the man had already killed Judge Craven.

She was only a few yards from the edge of the cliff now and could hear the water breaking on the rocks below. She crouched down, sheltered by several trees, and tried to get her breath. If she kept going in this direction, she'd back herself into a corner. The killer behind her. The treacherous cliff in front of her.

Gunfire rang out again. This time the bullet hit the tree trunk a foot above her head, splintering the bark and sending fragments flying into her face and hair. A trickle of blood ran down her cheek. She had to keep moving or he'd fire again, and this time he might be the lucky one.

It was a good ten feet to the next cluster of trees. She counted to three then took off running. The heel of her shoe caught on a root and she went sprawling into a bed of lacy ferns. Rolling over, she grabbed her ankle, which had twisted in the fall.

And then she felt something cold and hard jam into her back. She looked behind her and down the long, smooth barrel of a rifle.

"You shouldn't have done it, Callie. You shouldn't have brought Max Zirinsky into the game when it was almost over."

Judge Craven.

Only the man she knew had been transformed into someone she barely recognized. The muscles in his face were pulled tight, and his eyes had a wild look, as if he were on drugs or hallucinating. Callie was more certain now that he must be the one with the inoperable tumor, and the pressure from it was affecting his mind.

"Put the gun down, Judge Craven. Please, just put it down and let me help you."

"It's too late for that."

"No. It's not too late. I know about the tumor. You need medical care. Just put down the gun so that we can talk about it."

"No more talking. There's been enough of that."

"Think of Marjorie. You don't want her to see you like this. She loves you so much."

"Stop it."

He jabbed the barrel of the gun into her ribs again, and a sharp pain all but took her breath away. He was probably beyond reason, but she had to try.

"People respect you, Judge Craven," Callie said, forcing herself to suppress her own fear and keep her voice steady. "You uphold the law to the letter. You don't want to ruin the legacy of honesty and justice that you've created."

"There is no justice, Callie. Can't you see that? Can't anyone see that? No justice at all."

"You're probably right." Callie realized that she was only antagonizing a very unstable man. "Let's go back to the house and talk about it. It's so hot out here."

"No. I know what you're doing, but you can't stop me. I have a mission. I can't stop until it's finished. I can't stop until I make them pay." He stumbled backward, then caught himself, squinting his eyes as if he were having trouble focusing. "That's why I have to kill you, Callie. I can't let you stop me, no more than I could let Mary Hancock stop me." He straightened and his eyes took on a glassy stare as he pointed the gun at her chest.

"Please don't do this, Judge Craven. Think of Marjorie. This will destroy her. It will destroy you."

"It's too late to think of any of that. I've already been given the death sentence. A fatal brain tumor. It's payback for my sins. Payback for not making the guilty pay. This mission is my only redemption. I have no choice, Callie. You have to die."

He started blinking repetitively, then swayed forward, rolling onto the balls of his feet before rocking back on his heels. He'd gone totally mad, a victim himself of a ravaging disease and a distorted sense of justice.

Judge Lawrence Craven was the Avenger. He held his finger on the trigger, ready to kill again, and Callie was next on his list.

CHAPTER FIFTEEN

MAX STOPPED his questioning when a knock sounded on the door of the interrogation room. He stepped into the dimly lit hall. "Did you find out if Lawrence Craven was actually at Summarall and if he learned to shoot while he was there?"

"No, but I got something else you're gonna want to know about. Marjorie Craven just called. She found a body in her garden. She says it's an intern who came out to her house with Callie Baker. From the way she described him, I'd say it's Ted Gravier."

"Sonofabitch. Where's Callie?"

"Mrs. Craven doesn't know. Or if she does, I couldn't get it out of her. She's hysterical."

"What the hell was Ted doing taking Callie to the Cravens' in the middle of the day?"

"She was making a house call to check on Judge Craven, at least that's the message Ted left."

Max didn't wait to learn why he hadn't received the message. He took off for his car at a dead run. He couldn't bare to think that he might already be too late.

LAWRENCE CRAVEN'S right hand began to shake and his finger slid from the trigger. It wasn't much of a chance, but it might be the only one she got. Callie scrambled to her feet and took off running in a zigzagging path, the hammering in her chest so loud she wasn't sure she'd hear if a bullet was fired.

No problem. She not only heard the crack of gunfire but the sound of the bullet whizzing by her head. She kept running in the direction of the closest cover, a skimpy group of trees hugging the edge of the cliff. By the time she reached it, her lungs were burning, as if the oxygen she breathed was pure fire.

She fell against a tree trunk. Evidently Judge Craven's coordination had improved. Another shot rang out, and the bullet sprayed dirt a few feet in front of her. She took off running again, this time on the narrow path that separated the trees from the very edge of the cliff.

The bullets came faster now, as if Craven were shooting randomly. Callie had to keep moving and hope he gave up or someone came to help. Only there was no reason for anyone to come looking for her. Max thought she was in the hands of a capable cop and that the Avenger was at the police station with him.

Just then Callie lost her balance and grabbed for an overhanging branch to help her stay upright. When she missed, her left foot skidded in the dirt and slipped over the edge of the narrow path. Frantically she grabbed the spindly trunk of a tree growing out of the cliff and held on tightly.

As she struggled for a foothold, she felt both shoes go flying and she caught a quick flash of them sailing down to the rocks below. Panic threatened to overcome her. She couldn't hold on much longer. Then she'd follow the shoes, crashing onto the jagged rocks until a wave came in and washed her out to sea.

"Let go, Callie. Make it easy on both of us and just let go."

The judge's voice made her blood run cold. Either the obsession or the tumor had changed him into a demented demon.

"No. I won't make it easy, Lawrence. If you want me dead, then kill me like you did the others. But I'm innocent. You know that. I'm innocent, and I deserve to live."

His face contorted, he lifted his foot and the heel of his shoe slammed against her hand. Her fingers slipped, but so did Judge Craven.

She slid a good five feet before she managed to grab hold of a bush and stop her descent.

Judge Craven wasn't so lucky. His screams still reverberated in her mind and made her blood run cold as he plummeted to his death on the rocks below.

Or maybe he had been the lucky one, she decided as the roots of the bush began to give, showering her with clods of dirt. Judge Craven had died quickly, likely before he even knew what had happened. Maybe that's what he'd intended all along. To die while completing his mission rather than from an unrelenting tumor.

She couldn't hang on much longer, Callie realized. The Avenger would win after all.

She'd had one night with Max, and experienced a passion she'd never dreamed possible. But she wanted more. She wanted all life had to offer. She wanted to be Max's wife. To hold babies in her arms and rock them to sleep and kiss them good-night. She wanted to live. But she was going to die.

"Oh, Max. I love you. I should have told you that I love you." Now it was too late.

MAX STOOD AT THE EDGE of the cliff and stared down at the body smashed against the rocks. And then he spotted Callie, her eyes closed, her fingers clutched around the base of a stubby bush that was barely clinging to the cliffside. He raced over to her.

"Callie. It's Max. I'm here. Hold on, but don't move."

She opened her eyes and let her head fall back so that she could see above her. The movement caused more dirt to shake loose.

"Don't move, Callie. Just hold on. I'm climbing down to get you."

"No. You'll fall."

"No way."

He hoped he sounded a lot more confident than he felt as he searched for a foothold and crawled down one step at a time. If he had a rope, this would be a lot safer, but there was no time to go get one. He just had to take it slow and easy—but not too slow. He eased down one step more. He was close enough to grab her, but he needed something to support both their weight. Without it, they would plunge to their death.

No, he couldn't think that way. He wouldn't give up. A clod of dirt shifted beneath his foot.

"Nice day for rock climbing?"

Max looked up. Jerry Hawkins was standing there. The last man Max had expected to show up for a rescue, not that he was certain Jerry could do a thing to help.

"No use to do that the hard way," Jerry ripped his belt from his waist and dangled the length of black leather toward Max. "I'll hold on to that poor excuse of a tree there and brace myself. You grab the end of the belt and use it for support as you pull Callie up."

"Can you hold both of us?"

"Probably for longer than that spindly tree will bear our weight. So better make this quick."

Jerry took hold of the tree trunk, leaned down as far as he could and dangled the end of the belt within Max's reach. Max clutched it tightly with one hand and held on to Callie with the other. Using the belt like a support rope, he climbed the face of the cliff, barely breathing until they reached level ground.

Max took Callie in his arms and shuddered in relief as the sun beat down on them and the sirens of a half dozen police cars sounded in the distance, he was sure of only one thing.

Nothing in all his life had felt as good as holding Callie right now.

THE AVENGER WAS OFF the streets. His identity had stunned the whole town, just as Mary Hancock had predicted. Marjorie Craven had been the most shocked of all—and the most hurt. She insisted her husband's killing rampage had stemmed from the tumor, which must have affected his reasoning.

Max was no medical expert. He didn't know if she was right, and at this point, he didn't really care. If blaming all Judge Craven's problems on the tumor made it easier for his wife to accept what he'd done and the way he'd died, that was fine by Max. All that mattered to him was that the killings had stopped and the crimes were solved.

And most important of all, Callie was alive and safe. She was living alone in her beach house again. Max was in his apartment. Things were back to normal—as long as wanting her so badly he couldn't think straight was normal.

They hadn't talked since he'd held her in his arms on the edge of the cliff. That had been nearly forty-eight hours ago. But he was on his way to her house now, at her request, and he felt a wave of anticipation and apprehension.

His feelings for her had changed. He'd always been in love with her. But now that they'd made love, he couldn't imagine returning to the relationship they'd had before. He knew he couldn't go back to a pretense of mere friendship.

Yet he was still the same old Max, and he couldn't imagine that he'd fit into Callie's life any better now than before.

So where did that leave him except missing her every moment of every day for the rest of his life?

CALLIE SAT ACROSS the small deck table from Max as the sun took its final plunge into the Pacific. They'd discussed the Avenger case, Marjorie Craven's distress and even Gail Lodestrum's twins. They'd talked of everything except themselves or the future, or the fact that the world had all but stopped spinning when they'd made love.

Max finished off the can of beer he'd been nursing. "It's getting late. I guess I should go."

Callie took a deep breath of the salty air and reached across the table, sliding her hands over his. "I'd rather you didn't, Max."

His gaze met hers. She read the smoky desire in his eyes, but there was more. Questions. Maybe doubts.

"I'd love to stay, Callie. But I'm not good at this sort of thing. I can't just love a little bit or for a little while. I wish I could, but I can't."

"I didn't say anything about a time limit."

"Not yet, but I'm not the kind of guy who could fit in your life forever. Just look at me, and you'll know that."

"I am looking at you, Max, and I want to know one thing. Do you love me?"

He grimaced as if she'd hit him, but when his gaze met hers, she knew the answer even though he didn't say the words. And knowing that was all she needed.

"I don't care what you drink or how you dress or

what kind of hours you devote to your job. I only know that when we're together, I feel complete, and that what I feel for you isn't going away."

"I'd like to believe that, but..."

"No buts. I love you, Max. You. The way you are. And I'm not giving up on us, not even if it takes another eight years to get you back in my arms."

"That would be a hell of a long wait."

"So stay, Max. Give us a chance. That's all anyone ever has. We have to grab our happiness before it slips away and all we have of forever are regrets."

"Are you sure you know what you're asking?"

"Very, very sure. I love you."

"And I love you. I think I have since the very first night we met, loved you even when you were marrying someone else."

In seconds Callie was in his strong arms, and this time when Max's lips claimed hers, she knew that no matter what the future held, the true love she'd been afraid to hope for was here to stay.

EPILOGUE

Three months later:

"MY KIND OF WEDDING," Mikki announced. "Barefoot."

"I like the attire, too," Jerry said. "Of course, you look better in that sundress than I do in my shorts and this goofy Hawaiian shirt you bought me."

"I like that shirt."

"You would." He moved Seth to the other shoulder. "Just settle down, little guy. Your mom and dad are going to be marching down the beach any second now to tie the knot."

Sara started to fuss, so Mikki gave her a few pats on the back. "Do you actually think we're going to be able to manage the twins while Callie and Max are on their honeymoon?"

"Hey, the twins are yours. You're the baby expert. I'm taking Pickering."

"Not! You get diaper duty every night or no hanky panky when these two finally nod off to sleep."

"You drive a hard bargain."

"Oh, look, they're coming. Ohmigod. Callie is absolutely beautiful."

"Love does look good on her," Jerry agreed. "Looks good on Max, too. And they came so close to losing it all."

"Do you think they would have fallen if your mother hadn't sent you over to check on Marjorie when she did?"

"No way. Max would have found a way to save Callie. It was meant to be. But it *was* convenient I wore a belt that day."

"I knew they'd be a thing the first time I saw them together. And now everything's worked out. Callie and Max are together and Courage Bay can go back to being the beautiful, peaceful place it once was. Known for courage and not killers."

Jerry frowned. "Does that mean you're never going to marry me and move to Sacramento?"

"In due time, Mr. Hawkins. All in due time. Besides, that injury Callie was so concerned about isn't totally healed. You still need time to get over your partner's death. But right now it's time for a wedding, and I am going to cry."

CALLIE STOOD in what she was certain was the most beautiful spot on earth and stared into the eyes of the most magnificent man on the planet. There were no guests other than Mikki and Jerry and Gail's beautiful twins, whom Callie and Max were in the process of adopting.

The wedding was the way both she and Max had

wanted it. Simple. Beautiful. Perfect. Besides, if they'd started inviting guests, the list would have been endless, and the wedding would have been a monumental affair that would have been more for everyone else than for them.

Callie knew life wouldn't always be perfect. But if her experience with the Avenger had taught her anything, it was that life was precious and meant to be lived to the fullest.

She and Max exchanged their vows and the minister cleared his throat. "I now pronounce you Mr. and Mrs. Max Zirinsky. Max, you may kiss the bride."

Jerry and Mikki cheered. Pickering barked. Seth coughed. Sara cooed. Max kissed Callie and she kissed him right back. Beer or champagne, opera or the ball game, sushi or burgers, Callie and Max were a forever thing.

CODE RED

Ordinary People. Extraordinary Circumstances.

If you've enjoyed getting to know the men and women of California's Courage Bay Emergency Services team, Harlequin Books invites you to return to Courage Bay!

Just collect six (6) proofs of purchase from the back of six (6) different CODE RED titles and receive four (4) free CODE RED books that are not currently available in retail outlets!

Just complete the order form and send it, along with six (6) proofs of purchase from six (6) different CODE RED titles, to: CODE RED, P.O. Box 9047, Buffalo, NY 14269-9047, or P.O. Box 613, Fort Erie, Ontario L2A 5X3. (Cost of $2.00 for shipping and handling applies.)

Name (PLEASE PRINT)

Address   Apt. #

City   State/Prov.   Zip/Postal Code

093 KKA DXH7

When you return six proofs of purchase, you will receive the following titles:

RIDING THE STORM by Julie Miller	**TURBULENCE** by Jessica Matthews
WASHED AWAY by Carol Marinelli	**HARD RAIN** by Darlene Scalera

To receive your free CODE RED books (retail value $19.96), complete the above form. Mail it to us with six proofs of purchase, one of which can be found in the right-hand corner of this page. Requests must be received no later than October 31, 2005. Your set of four CODE RED books costs you only $2.00 shipping and handling. N.Y. state residents must add applicable sales tax on shipping and handling charge. Please allow 6–8 weeks for receipt of order. Offer good in Canada and U.S. only. Offer good while quantities last.

When you respond to this offer, we will also send you *Inside Romance*, a free quarterly publication, highlighting upcoming releases and promotions from Harlequin and Silhouette Books.

☐ If you do not wish to receive this free publication, please check here.

CODE **RED**

ONE PROOF OF PURCHASE

CRPOP12

MINISERIES

Coming in August...

USA TODAY bestselling author

Dixie Browning

LAWLESS LOVERS

Two complete novels from
The Lawless Heirs saga.

Daniel Lyon Lawless and Harrison Lawless are two
successful, sexy and very sought after bachelors.
But their worlds are about to be rocked by the
love of two headstrong, beautiful women!

**Bonus Features,
including:**

The Writing Life,

Family Tree

and Sneak Peek
from a NEW Lawless
Heirs title coming
in September!

Where love comes alive™

SAGA

Coming in August…

**A dramatic new story in
The Bachelors of Blair Memorial saga…**

USA TODAY bestselling author

Marie Ferrarella

SEARCHING
FOR CATE

A widower for three years, Dr. Christian Graywolf
knows his life is his work at Blair Memorial Hospital.
But when he meets FBI special agent Cate Kowalski—
a woman searching for her birth mother—the attraction
is intense and immediate. And the truth is something
neither Christian nor Cate expects—that all his life
Christian has been searching for Cate.

**Bonus Features,
including:
Sneak Peek,
The Writing Life
and Family Tree**

Where love comes alive™

If you enjoyed what you just read,
then we've got an offer you can't resist!

Take 2 bestselling novels FREE!
Plus get a FREE surprise gift!

Clip this page and mail it to MIRA®

IN U.S.A.
3010 Walden Ave.
P.O. Box 1867
Buffalo, N.Y. 14240-1867

IN CANADA
P.O. Box 609
Fort Erie, Ontario
L2A 5X3

YES! Please send me 2 free MIRA® novels and my free surprise gift. After receiving them, if I don't wish to receive anymore, I can return the shipping statement marked cancel. If I don't cancel, I will receive 4 brand-new novels every month, before they're available in stores! In the U.S.A., bill me at the bargain price of $4.99 plus 25¢ shipping and handling per book and applicable sales tax, if any*. In Canada, bill me at the bargain price of $5.49 plus 25¢ shipping and handling per book and applicable taxes**. That's the complete price and a savings of over 20% off the cover prices—what a great deal! I understand that accepting the 2 free books and gift places me under no obligation ever to buy any books. I can always return a shipment and cancel at any time. Even if I never buy another The Best of the Best™ book, the 2 free books and gift are mine to keep forever.

185 MDN DZ7J
385 MDN DZ7K

Name	(PLEASE PRINT)	
Address	Apt.#	
City	State/Prov.	Zip/Postal Code

*Not valid to current The Best of the Best™, Mira®,
suspense and romance subscribers.*

**Want to try two free books from another series?
Call 1-800-873-8635 or visit www.morefreebooks.com.**

* Terms and prices subject to change without notice. Sales tax applicable in N.Y.
** Canadian residents will be charged applicable provincial taxes and GST.
All orders subject to approval. Offer limited to one per household.
® and ™are registered trademarks owned and used by the trademark owner and or its licensee.

BOB04R   ©2004 Harlequin Enterprises Limited

SPOTLIGHT

HAPPILY NEVER AFTER

A modern Gothic tale set in a small New England town.

National bestselling author

Kathleen O'Brien

Ten years after the society wedding that wasn't, members of the wedding party are starting to die. At the scene of every "accident," a piece of a wedding dress is found. It's not long before Kelly Ralston realizes that she's the sole remaining bridesmaid left…and the next target!

Available in August.

Exclusive Bonus Features:

Author Interview

Map

and MORE!

Where love comes alive™